NANCY DREW

#18 *girl detective* ®

City Under the Basement

STEFAN PETRUCHA & SARAH KINNEY • Writers
SHO MURASE • Artist
with 3D CG elements and color by CARLOS JOSE GUZMAN
Based on the series by
CAROLYN KEENE

PAPERCUT Z ™
New York

City Under the Basement
STEFAN PETRUCHA & SARAH KINNEY – Writers
SHO MURASE – Artist
with 3D CG elements and color by CARLOS JOSE GUZMAN
BRYAN SENKA – Letterer
MIKHAELA REID and MASHEKA WOOD – Production
MICHAEL PETRANEK - Editorial Assistant
JIM SALICRUP
Editor-in-Chief

ISBN 10: 1-59707-154-4 paperback edition
ISBN 13: 978-1-59707-154-3 paperback edition
ISBN 10: 1-59707-155-2 hardcover edition
ISBN 13: 978-1-59707-155-0 hardcover edition

Printed in China.
April 2009 by WKT Co. LTD.
3/F Phase I Leader Industrial Centre
188 Texaco Road, Tseun Wan, N.T.
Hong Kong

Distributed by Macmillan.

10   9   8   7   6   5   4   3   2   1

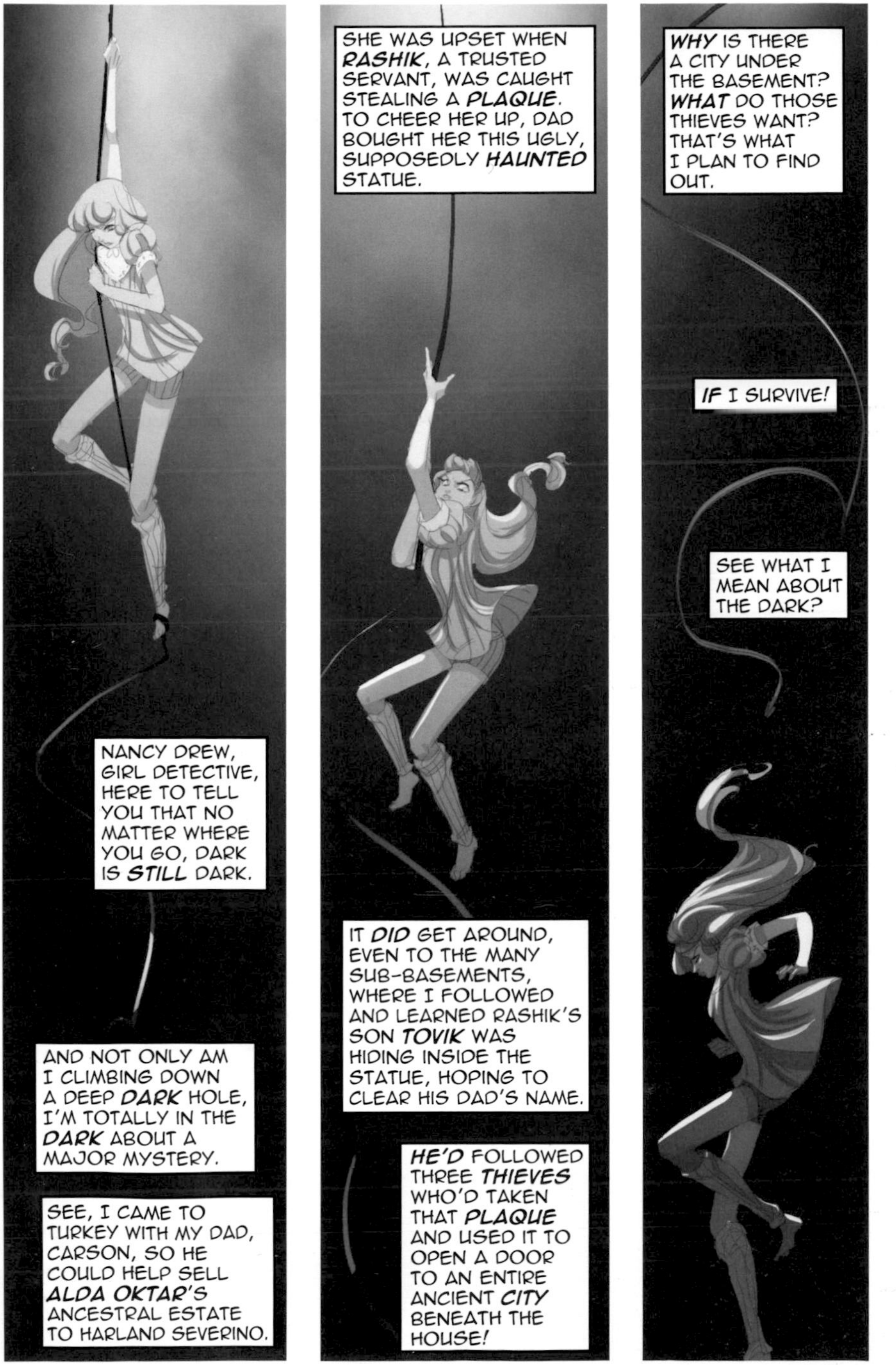
NANCY DREW, GIRL DETECTIVE, HERE TO TELL YOU THAT NO MATTER WHERE YOU GO, DARK IS STILL DARK.
AND NOT ONLY AM I CLIMBING DOWN A DEEP DARK HOLE, I'M TOTALLY IN THE DARK ABOUT A MAJOR MYSTERY.
SEE, I CAME TO TURKEY WITH MY DAD, CARSON, SO HE COULD HELP SELL ALDA OKTAR'S ANCESTRAL ESTATE TO HARLAND SEVERINO.
SHE WAS UPSET WHEN RASHIK, A TRUSTED SERVANT, WAS CAUGHT STEALING A PLAQUE. TO CHEER HER UP, DAD BOUGHT HER THIS UGLY, SUPPOSEDLY HAUNTED STATUE.
IT DID GET AROUND, EVEN TO THE MANY SUB-BASEMENTS, WHERE I FOLLOWED AND LEARNED RASHIK'S SON TOVIK WAS HIDING INSIDE THE STATUE, HOPING TO CLEAR HIS DAD'S NAME.
HE'D FOLLOWED THREE THIEVES WHO'D TAKEN THAT PLAQUE AND USED IT TO OPEN A DOOR TO AN ENTIRE ANCIENT CITY BENEATH THE HOUSE!
WHY IS THERE A CITY UNDER THE BASEMENT? WHAT DO THOSE THIEVES WANT? THAT'S WHAT I PLAN TO FIND OUT.
IF I SURVIVE!
SEE WHAT I MEAN ABOUT THE DARK?

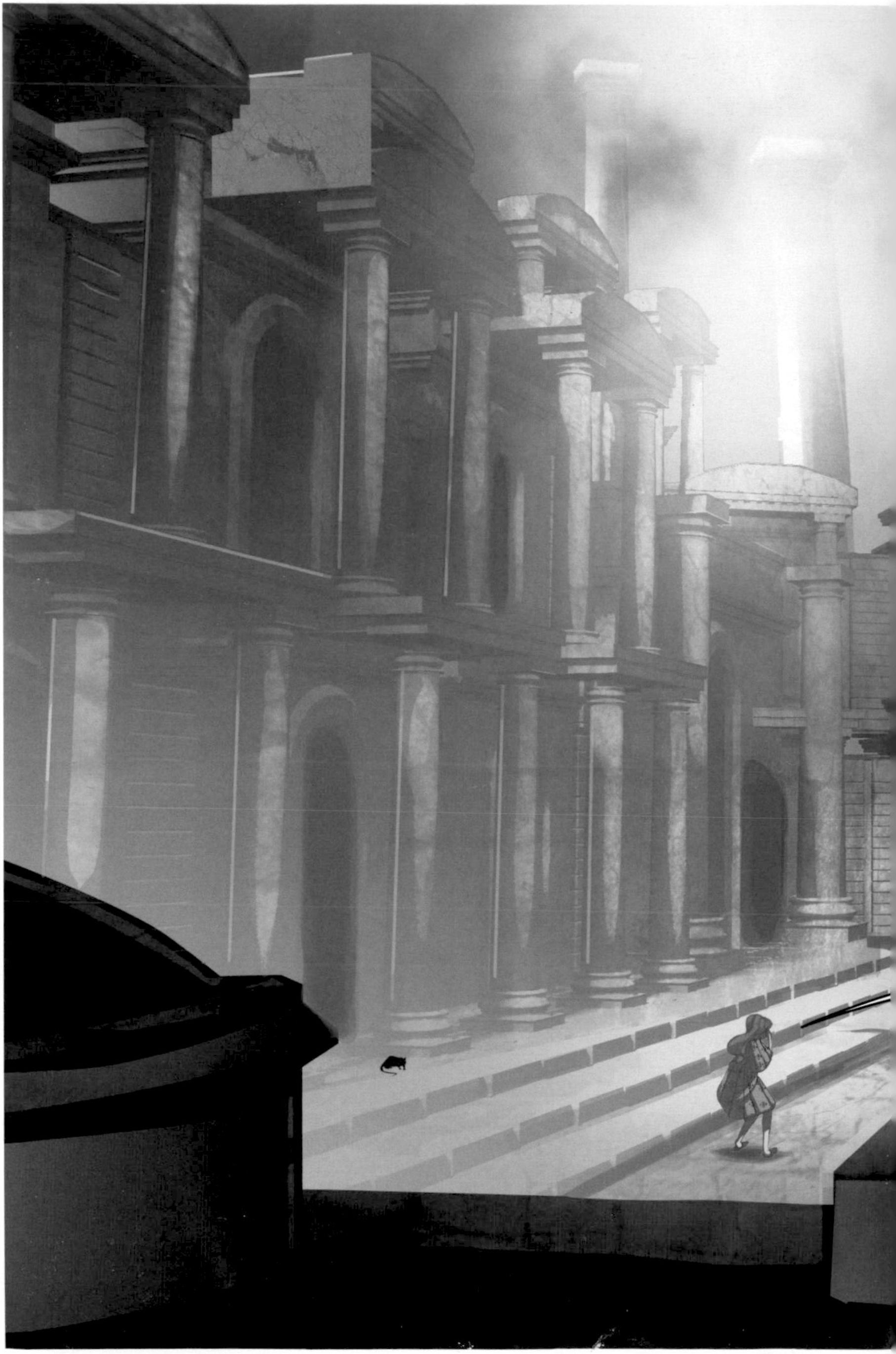

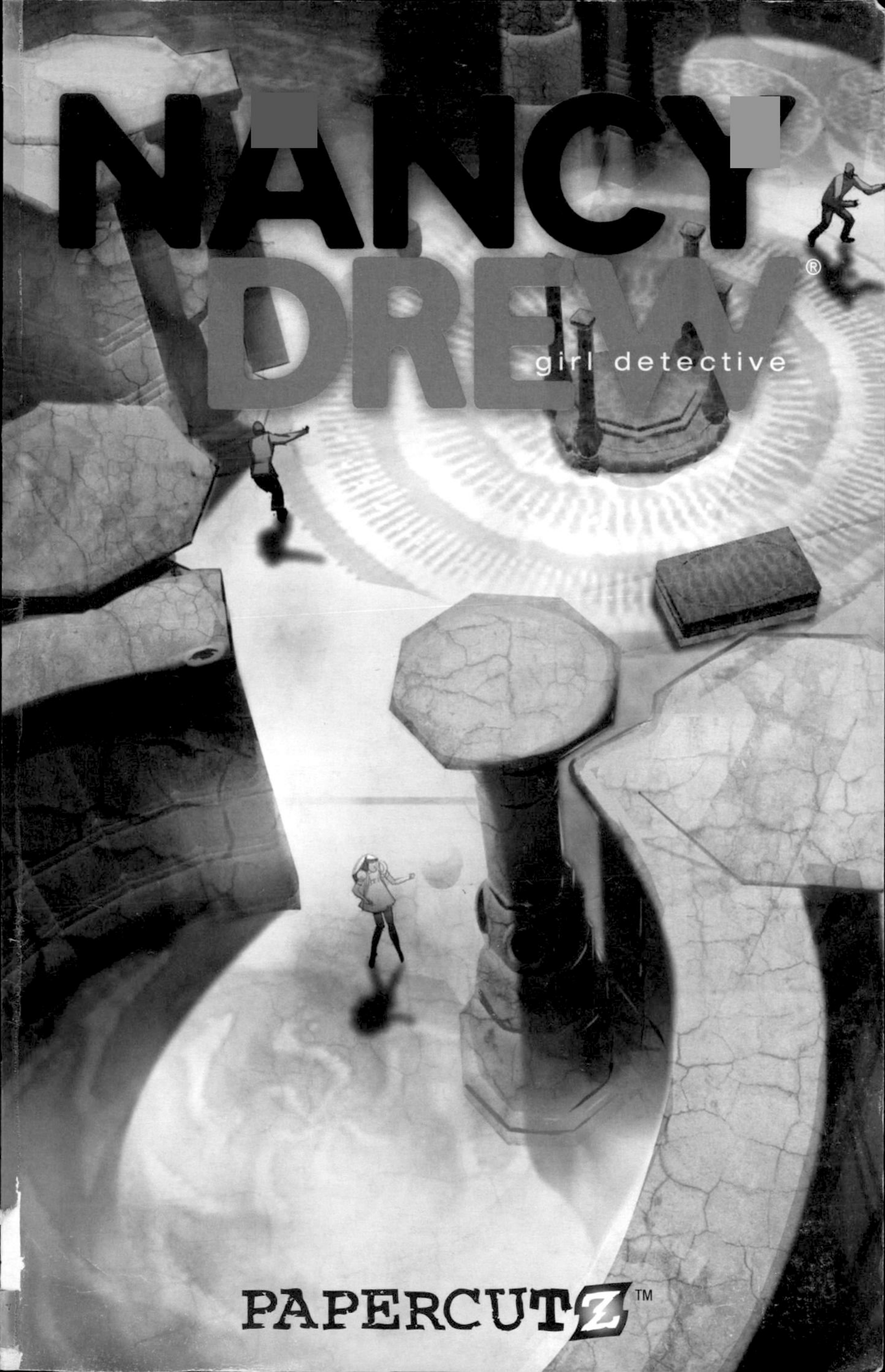
NANCY DREW®
girl detective
PAPERCUTZ™

NANCY DREW GRAPHIC NOVELS AVAILABLE FROM PAPERCUTZ

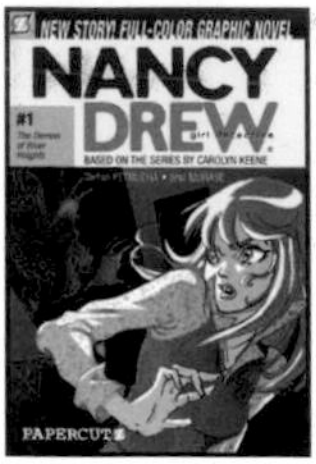
NEW STORY! FULL-COLOR GRAPHIC NOVEL
NANCY
DREW
PAPERCUTZ

#1 "The Demon of River Heights"

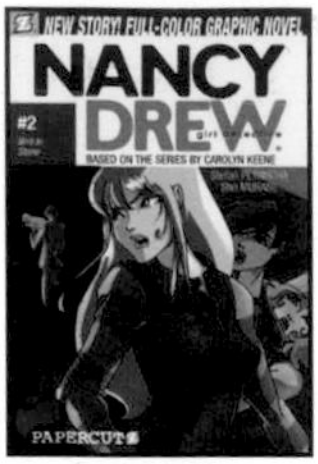
NEW STORY! FULL-COLOR GRAPHIC NOVEL
NANCY
DREW
PAPERCUTZ

#2 "Writ In Stone"

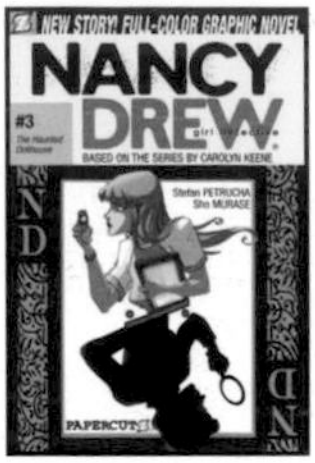
NEW STORY! FULL-COLOR GRAPHIC NOVEL
NANCY
DREW
PAPERCUTZ

#3 "The Haunted Dollhouse"

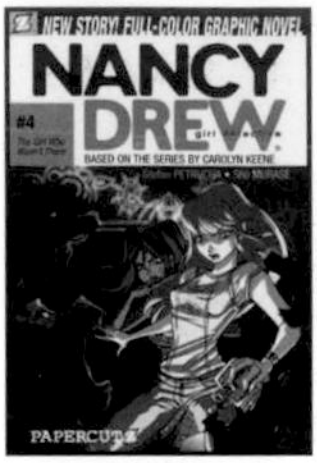
NEW STORY! FULL-COLOR GRAPHIC NOVEL
NANCY
DREW
PAPERCUTZ

#4 "The Girl Who Wasn't There"

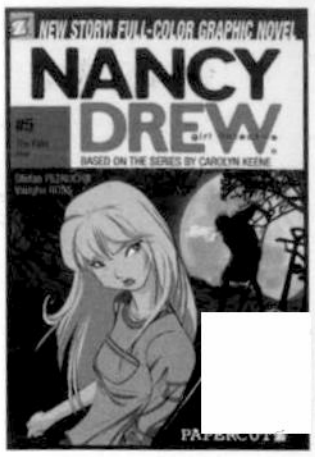
NEW STORY! FULL-COLOR GRAPHIC NOVEL
NANCY
DREW

#5 "The Fake Heir"

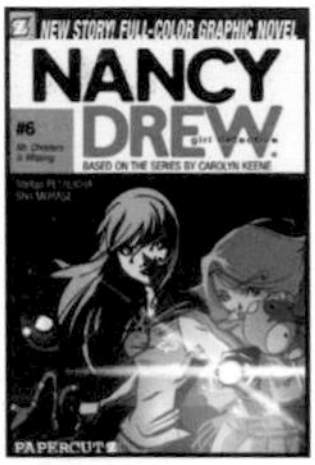
NEW STORY! FULL-COLOR GRAPHIC NOVEL
NANCY
DREW
PAPERCUTZ

#6 "Mr. Cheeters Is Missing"

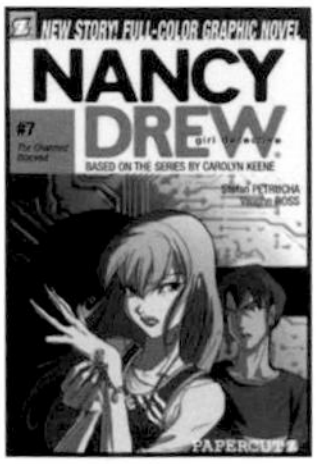
NEW STORY! FULL-COLOR GRAPHIC NOVEL
NANCY
DREW
PAPERCUTZ

#7 "The Charmed Bracelet"

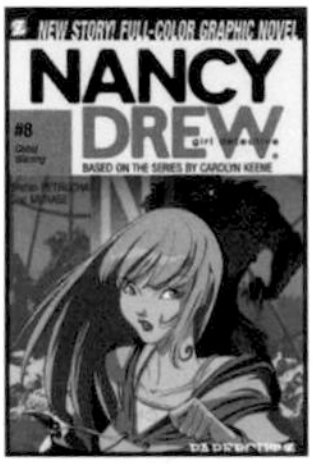
NEW STORY! FULL-COLOR GRAPHIC NOVEL
NANCY
DREW

#8 "Global Warning"

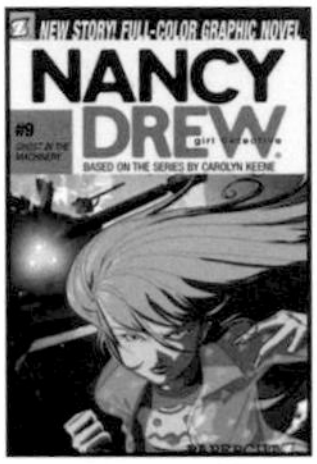
NEW STORY! FULL-COLOR GRAPHIC NOVEL
NANCY
DREW

#9 "Ghost In The Machinery"

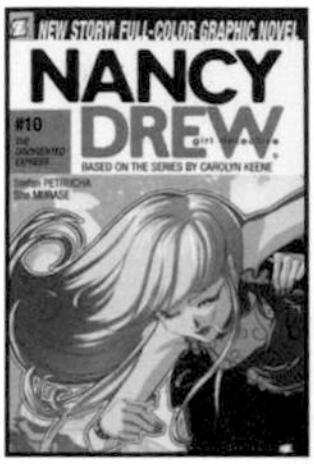
NEW STORY! FULL-COLOR GRAPHIC NOVEL
NANCY
DREW

#10 "The Disoriented Express"

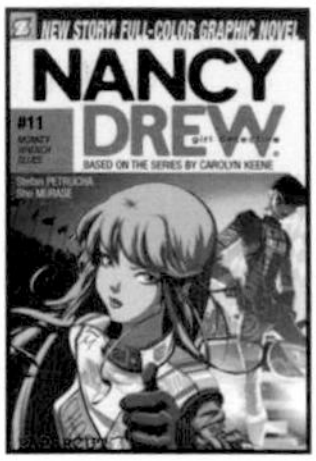
NEW STORY! FULL-COLOR GRAPHIC NOVEL
NANCY
DREW

#11 "Monkey Wrench Blues"

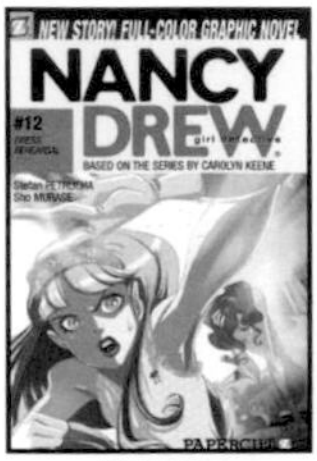
NEW STORY! FULL-COLOR GRAPHIC NOVEL
NANCY
DREW

#12 "Dress Reversal"

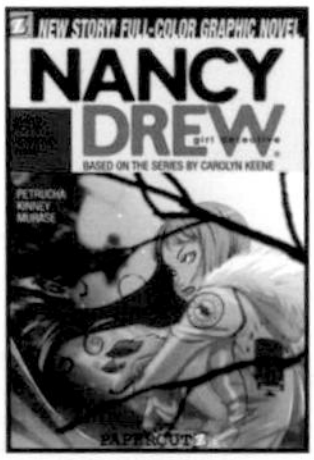
NEW STORY! FULL-COLOR GRAPHIC NOVEL
NANCY
DREW
PAPERCUTZ

#13 "Doggone Town"

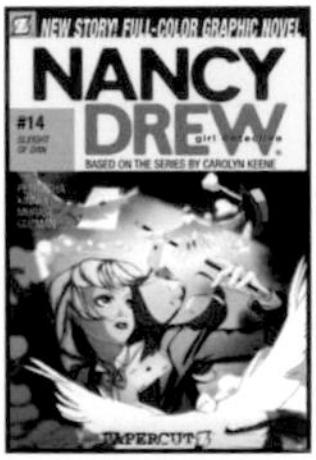
NEW STORY! FULL-COLOR GRAPHIC NOVEL
NANCY
DREW
PAPERCUTZ

#14 "Sleight of Dan"

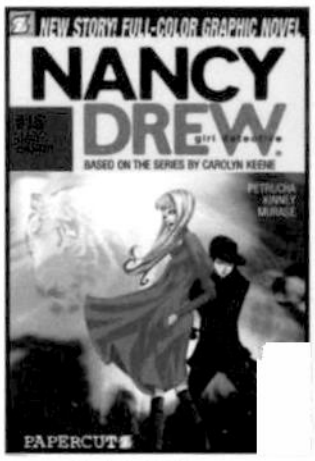
NEW STORY! FULL-COLOR GRAPHIC NOVEL
NANCY
DREW
PAPERCUTZ

#15 "Tiger Counter"

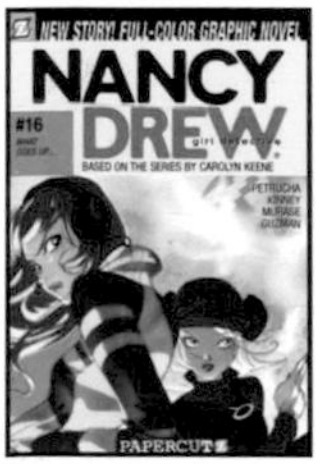
NEW STORY! FULL-COLOR GRAPHIC NOVEL
NANCY
DREW
PAPERCUTZ

#16 "What Goes Up..."

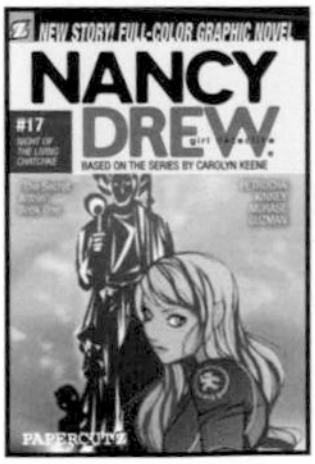
NEW STORY! FULL-COLOR GRAPHIC NOVEL
NANCY
DREW
PAPERCUTZ

#17 "Night of the Living Chatchke"

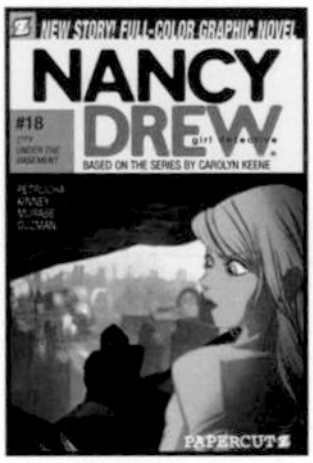
NEW STORY! FULL-COLOR GRAPHIC NOVEL
NANCY
DREW
PAPERCUTZ

#18 "City Under the Basement"

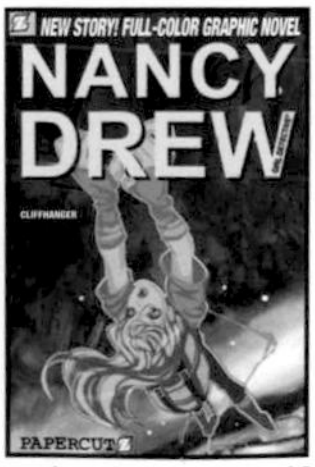
NEW STORY! FULL-COLOR GRAPHIC NOVEL
NANCY
DREW
CLIFFHANGER
PAPERCUTZ

Coming November '09
#19 "Cliffhanger"

$7.95 each in paperback, $12.95 each in hardcover. Please add $4.00 for postage and handling for the first book, add $1.00 for each additional book. Please make check payable to NBM Publishing. Send to:

Papercutz, 40 Exchange Place, Suite 1308, New York, NY 10005, 1-800-886-1223

www.papercutz.com

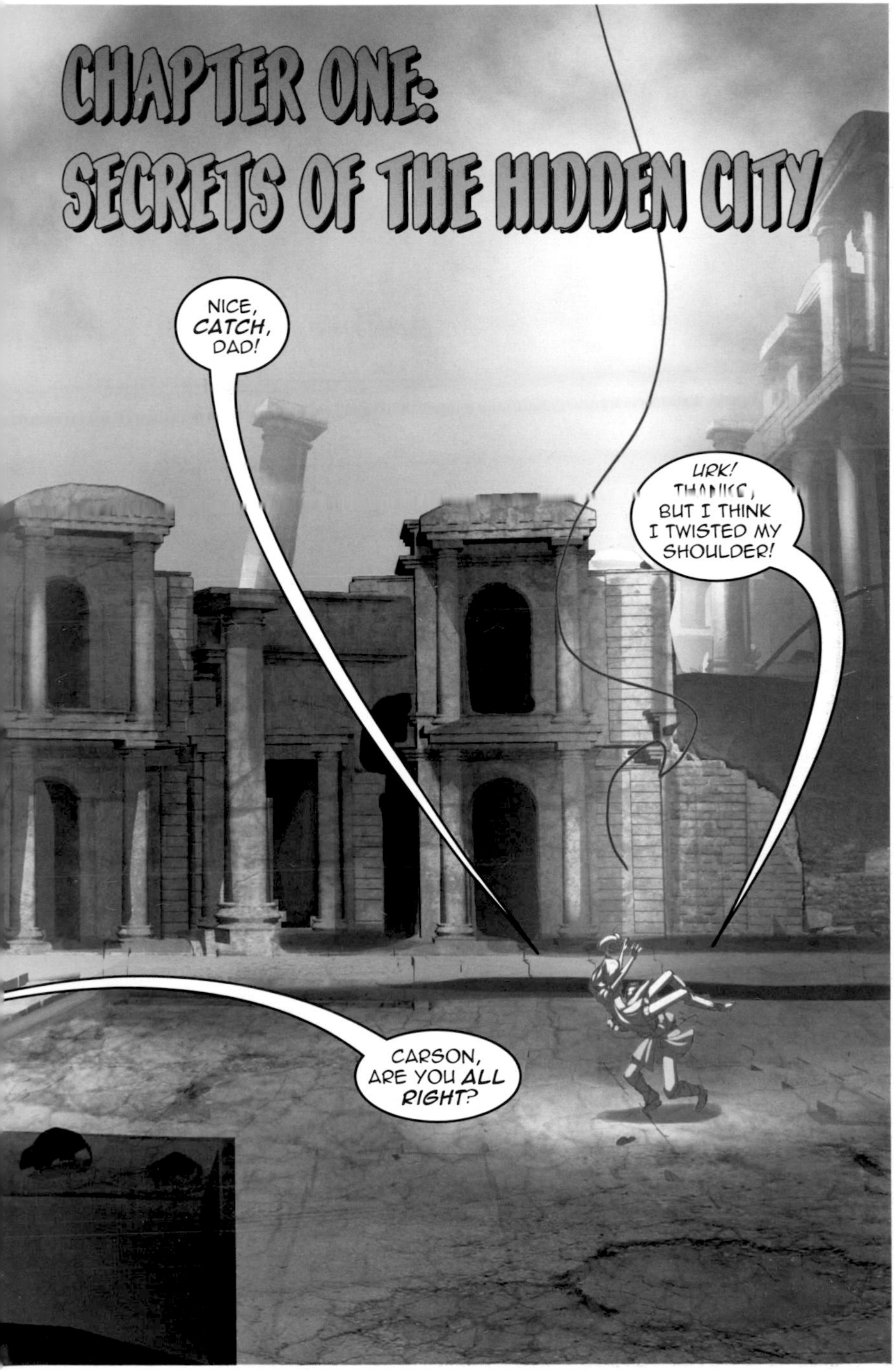
CHAPTER ONE:
SECRETS OF THE HIDDEN CITY
NICE, CATCH, DAD!
URK! BUT I THINK I TWISTED MY SHOULDER!
CARSON, ARE YOU ALL RIGHT?

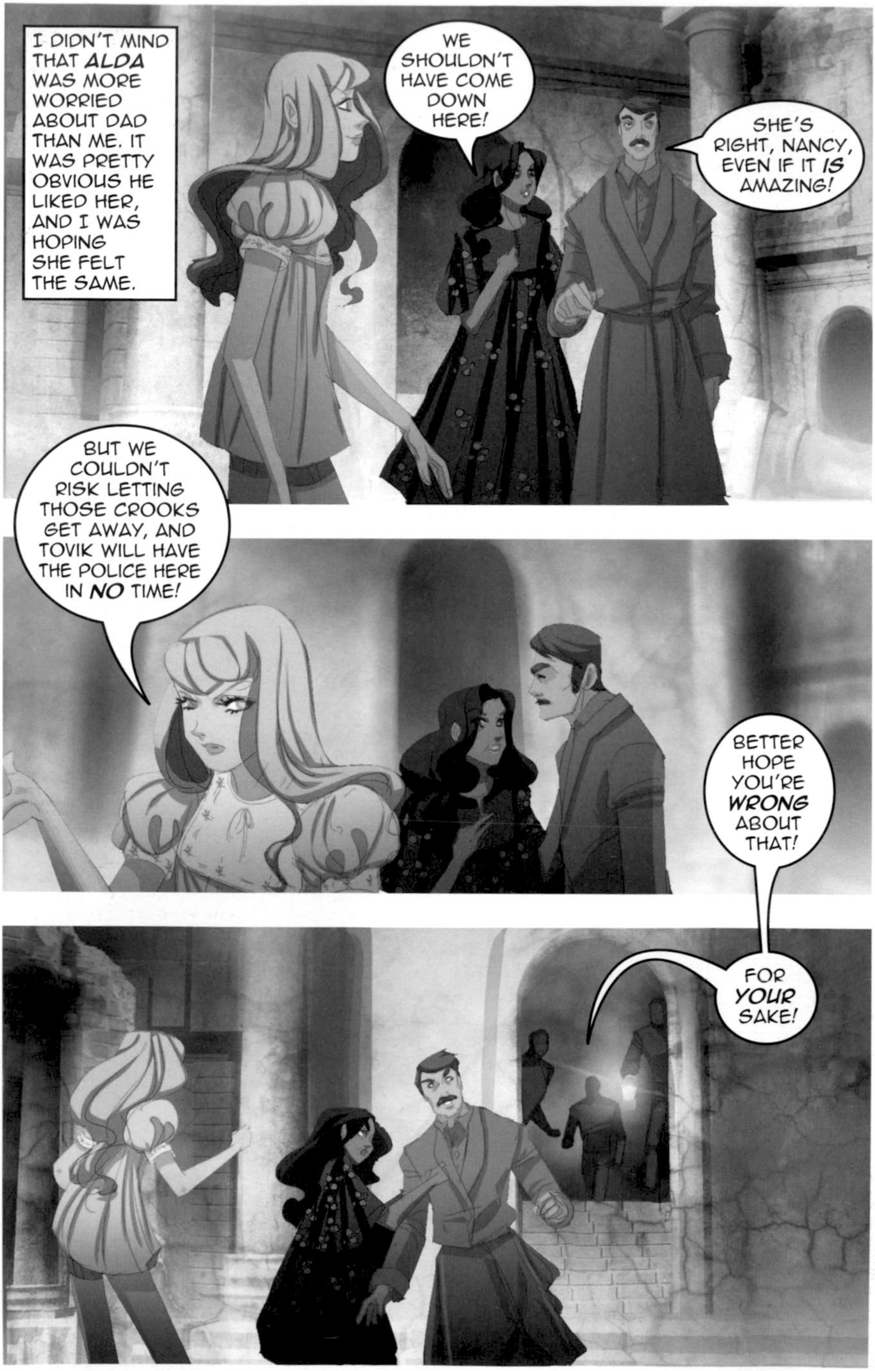
I DIDN'T MIND THAT ALDA WAS MORE WORRIED ABOUT DAD THAN ME. IT WAS PRETTY OBVIOUS HE LIKED HER, AND I WAS HOPING SHE FELT THE SAME.
WE SHOULDN'T HAVE COME DOWN HERE!
SHE'S RIGHT, NANCY, EVEN IF IT IS AMAZING!
BUT WE COULDN'T RISK LETTING THOSE CROOKS GET AWAY, AND TOVIK WILL HAVE THE POLICE HERE IN NO TIME!
BETTER HOPE YOU'RE WRONG ABOUT THAT!
FOR YOUR SAKE!

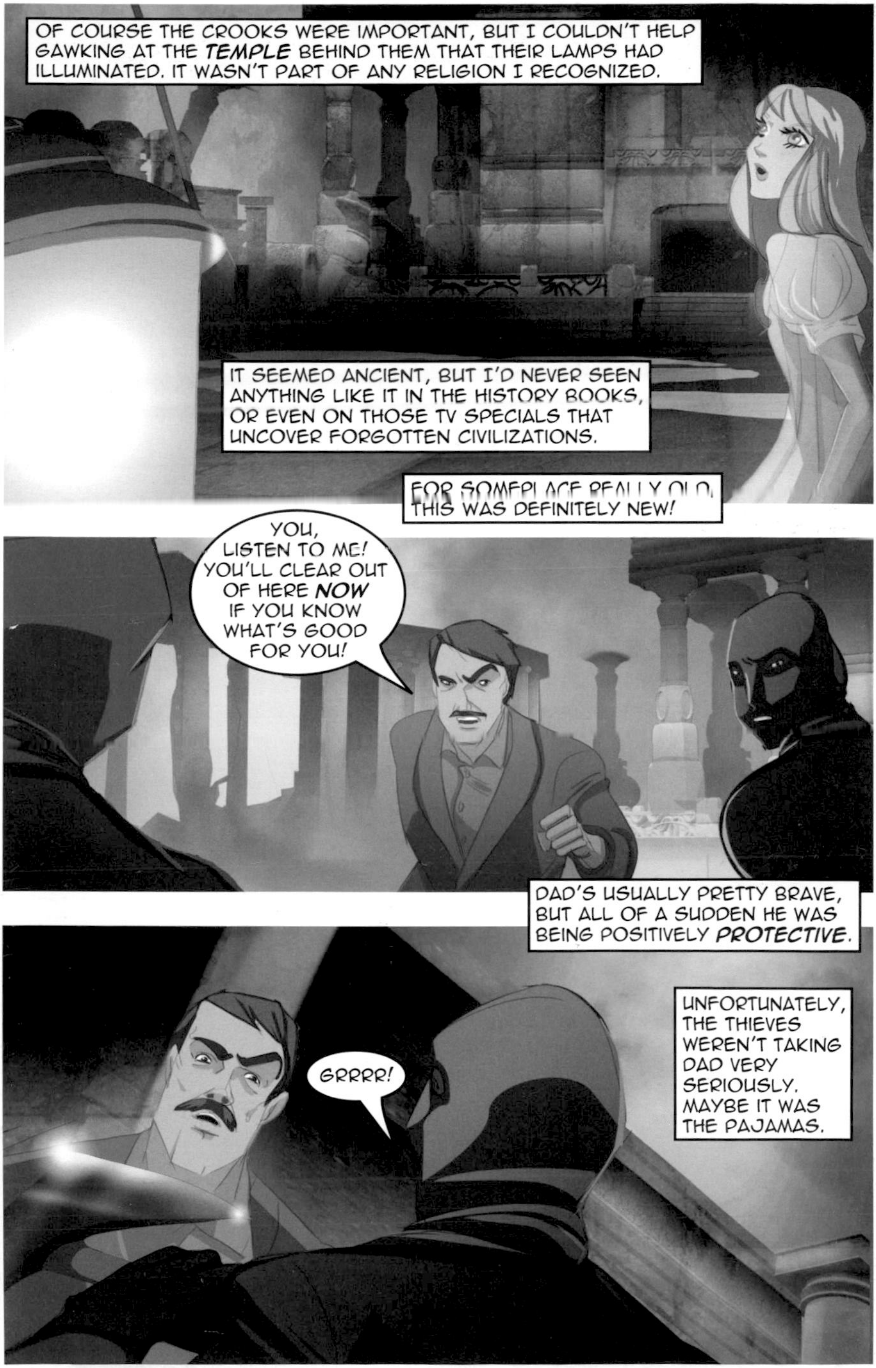
OF COURSE THE CROOKS WERE IMPORTANT, BUT I COULDN'T HELP GAWKING AT THE *TEMPLE* BEHIND THEM THAT THEIR LAMPS HAD ILLUMINATED. IT WASN'T PART OF ANY RELIGION I RECOGNIZED.
IT SEEMED ANCIENT, BUT I'D NEVER SEEN ANYTHING LIKE IT IN THE HISTORY BOOKS, OR EVEN ON THOSE TV SPECIALS THAT UNCOVER FORGOTTEN CIVILIZATIONS.
FOR SOMEPLACE REALLY OLD, THIS WAS DEFINITELY NEW!
YOU, LISTEN TO ME! YOU'LL CLEAR OUT OF HERE ***NOW*** IF YOU KNOW WHAT'S GOOD FOR YOU!
DAD'S USUALLY PRETTY BRAVE, BUT ALL OF A SUDDEN HE WAS BEING POSITIVELY ***PROTECTIVE***.
UNFORTUNATELY, THE THIEVES WEREN'T TAKING DAD VERY SERIOUSLY. MAYBE IT WAS THE PAJAMAS.
GRRRR!

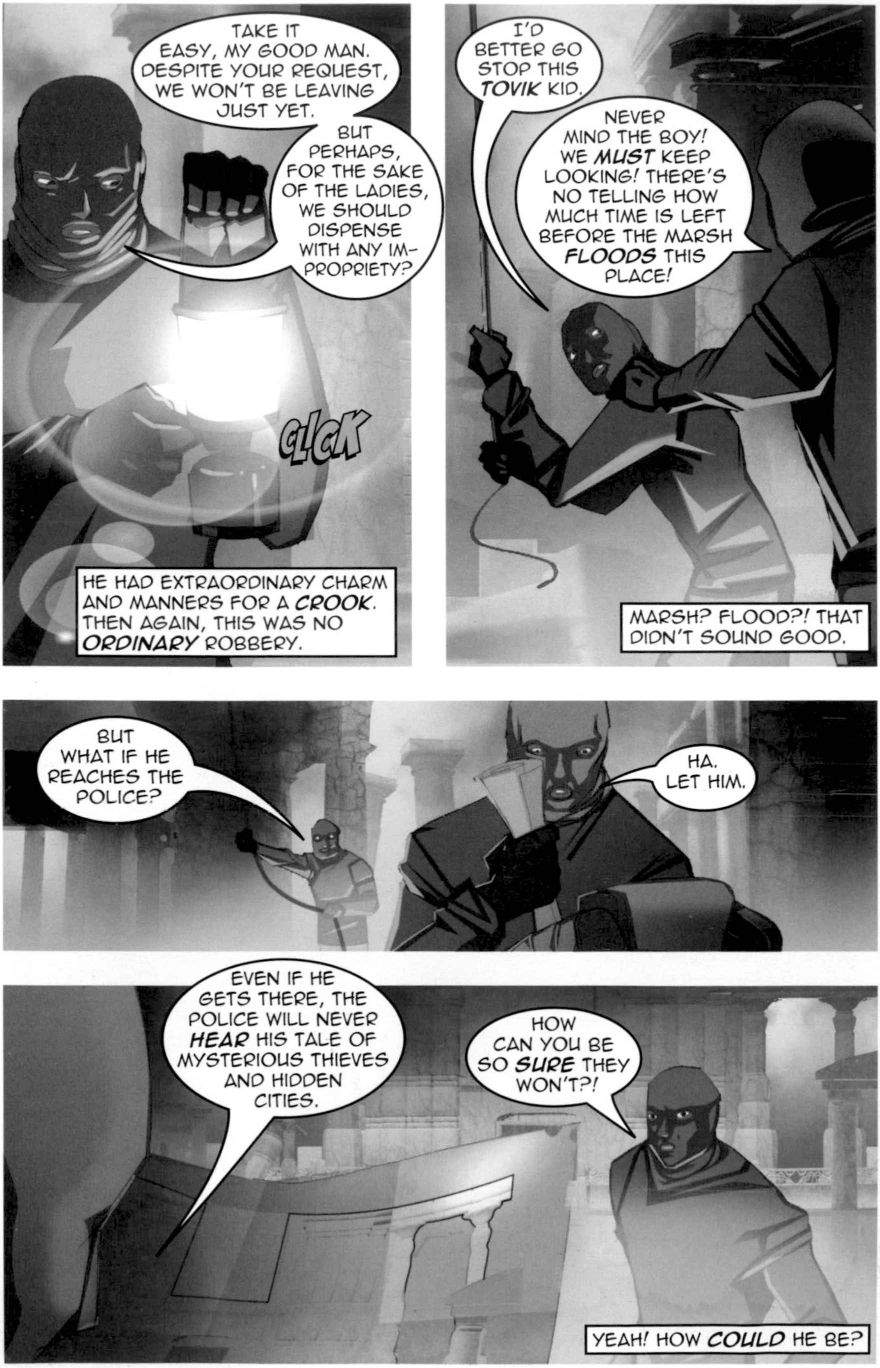
TAKE IT EASY, MY GOOD MAN. DESPITE YOUR REQUEST, WE WON'T BE LEAVING JUST YET.
BUT PERHAPS, FOR THE SAKE OF THE LADIES, WE SHOULD DISPENSE WITH ANY IM-PROPRIETY?
CLICK
HE HAD EXTRAORDINARY CHARM AND MANNERS FOR A CROOK. THEN AGAIN, THIS WAS NO ORDINARY ROBBERY.
I'D BETTER GO STOP THIS TOVIK KID.
NEVER MIND THE BOY! WE MUST KEEP LOOKING! THERE'S NO TELLING HOW MUCH TIME IS LEFT BEFORE THE MARSH FLOODS THIS PLACE!
MARSH? FLOOD?! THAT DIDN'T SOUND GOOD.
BUT WHAT IF HE REACHES THE POLICE?
HA. LET HIM.
EVEN IF HE GETS THERE, THE POLICE WILL NEVER HEAR HIS TALE OF MYSTERIOUS THIEVES AND HIDDEN CITIES.
HOW CAN YOU BE SO SURE THEY WON'T?!
YEAH! HOW COULD HE BE?

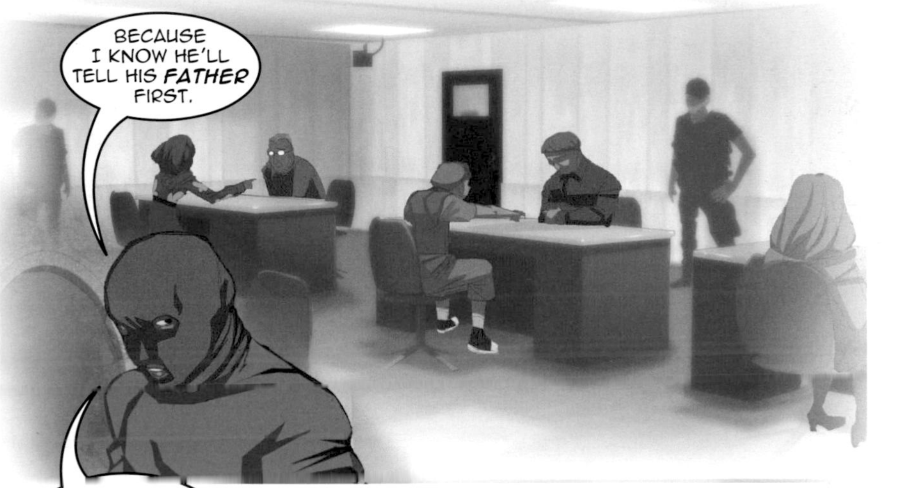
BECAUSE I KNOW HE'LL TELL HIS *FATHER* FIRST.

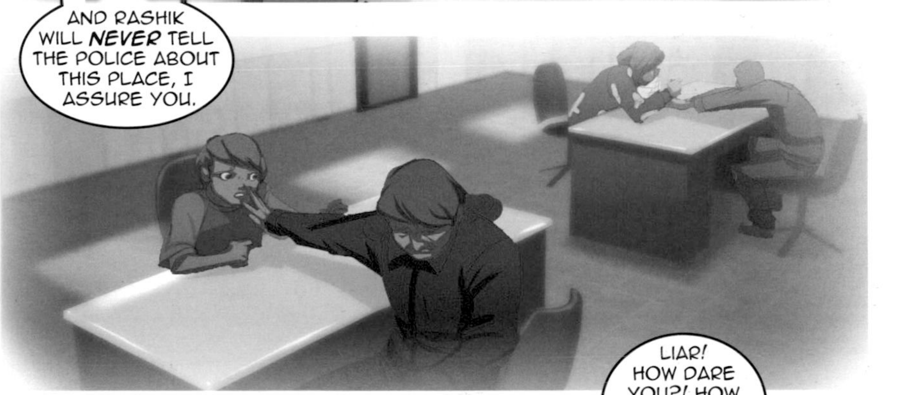
AND RASHIK WILL *NEVER* TELL THE POLICE ABOUT THIS PLACE, I ASSURE YOU.

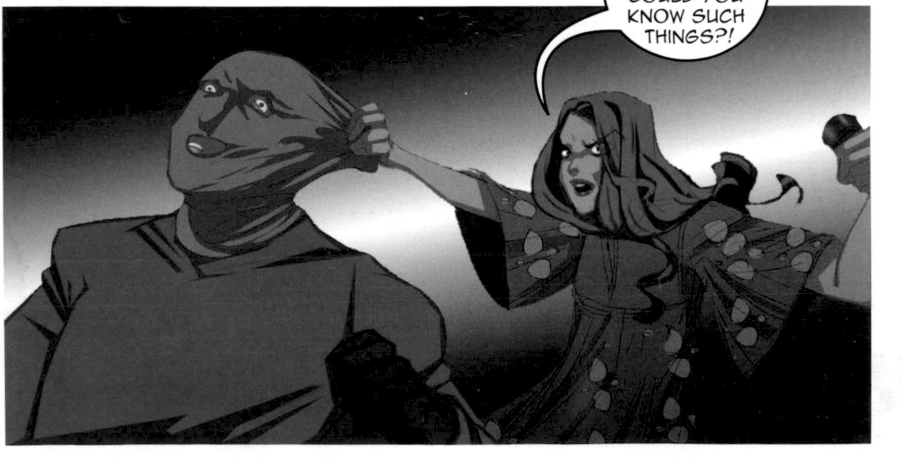
LIAR! HOW DARE YOU?! HOW COULD YOU KNOW SUCH THINGS?!

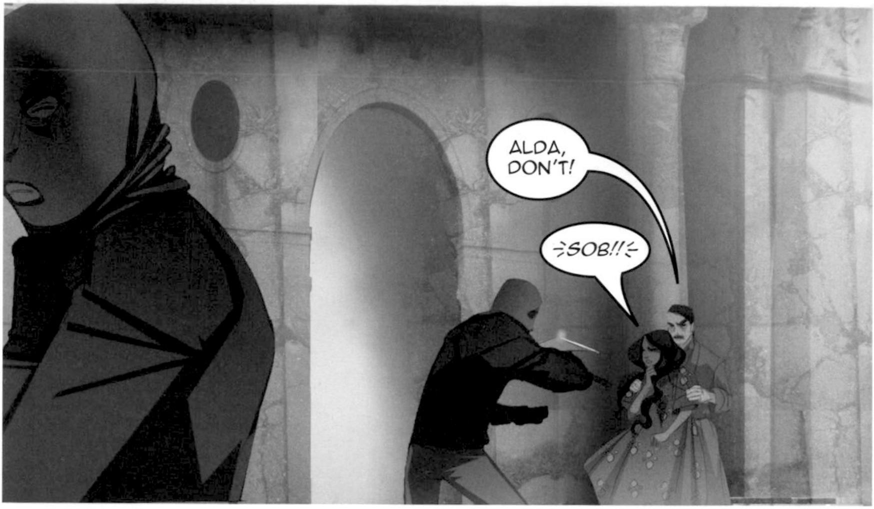
ALDA, DON'T!
SOB!!

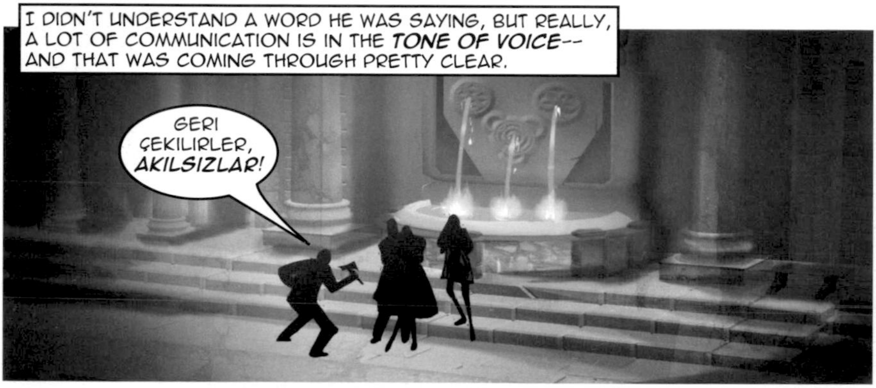
I DIDN'T UNDERSTAND A WORD HE WAS SAYING, BUT REALLY, A LOT OF COMMUNICATION IS IN THE TONE OF VOICE-- AND THAT WAS COMING THROUGH PRETTY CLEAR.
GERI ÇEKILIRLER, AKILSIZLAR!

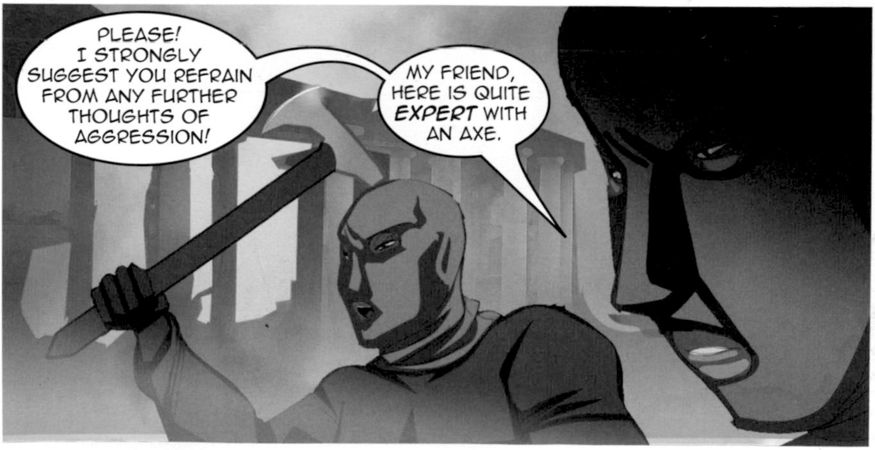
PLEASE! I STRONGLY SUGGEST YOU REFRAIN FROM ANY FURTHER THOUGHTS OF AGGRESSION!
MY FRIEND, HERE IS QUITE EXPERT WITH AN AXE.

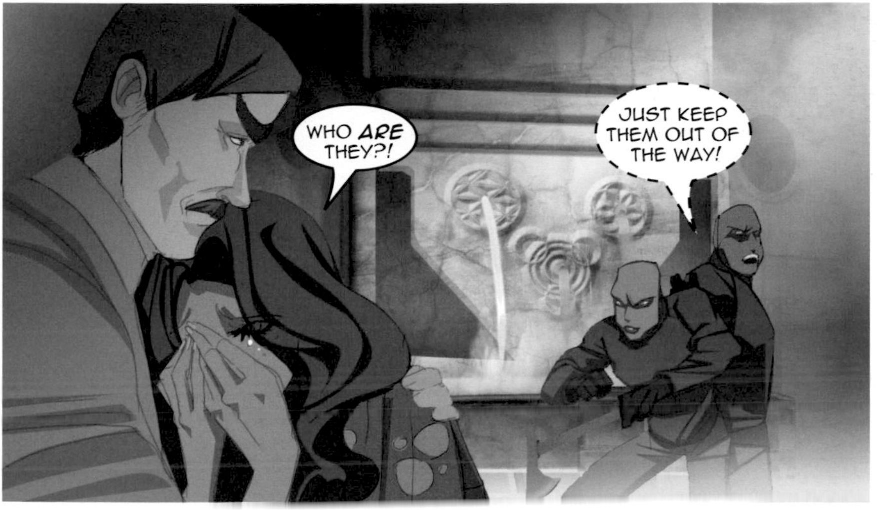
WHO *ARE* THEY?!
JUST KEEP THEM OUT OF THE WAY!

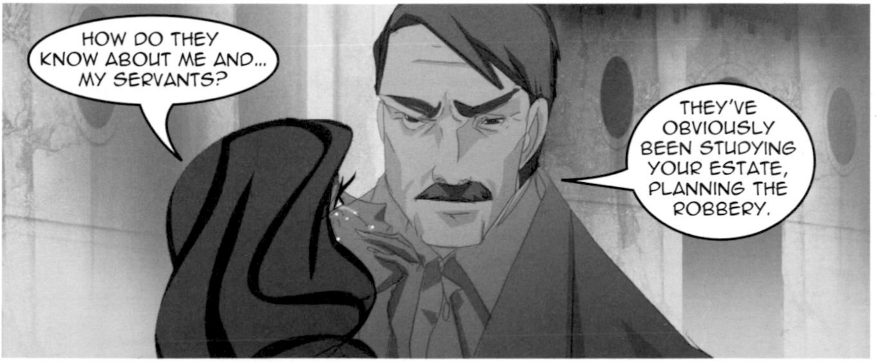
HOW DO THEY KNOW ABOUT ME AND... MY SERVANTS?
THEY'VE OBVIOUSLY BEEN STUDYING YOUR ESTATE, PLANNING THE ROBBERY.

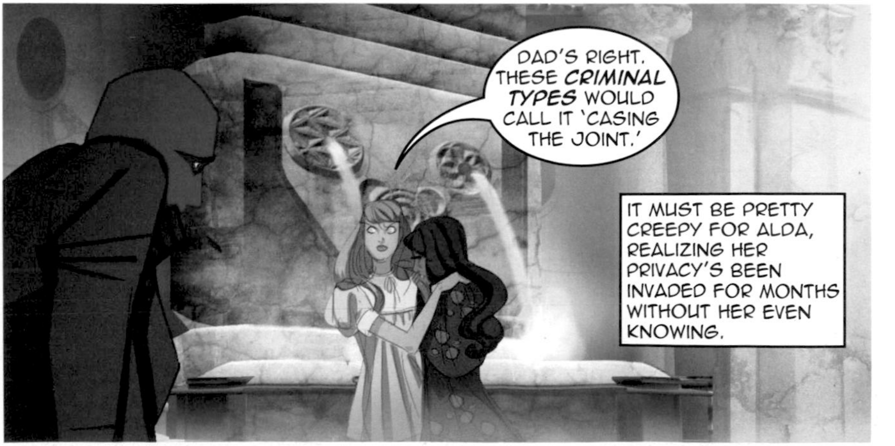
DAD'S RIGHT. THESE *CRIMINAL TYPES* WOULD CALL IT 'CASING THE JOINT.'
IT MUST BE PRETTY CREEPY FOR ALDA, REALIZING HER PRIVACY'S BEEN INVADED FOR MONTHS WITHOUT HER EVEN KNOWING.

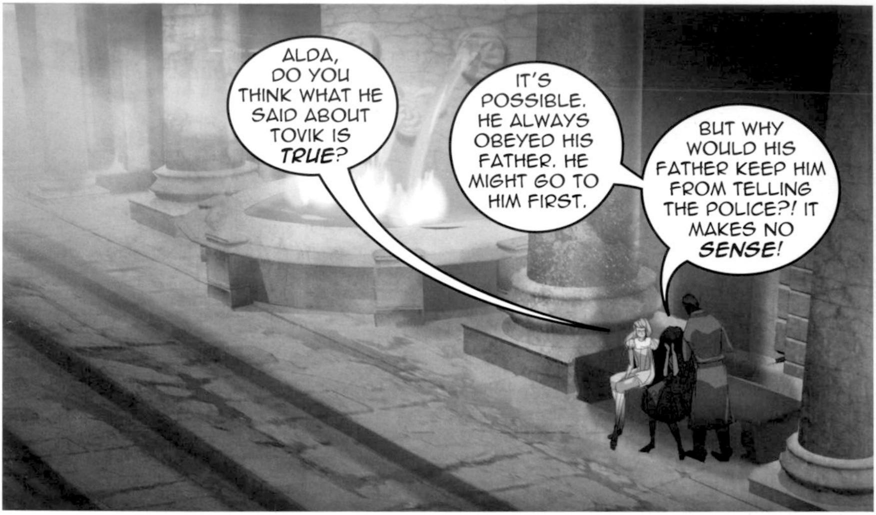
ALDA, DO YOU THINK WHAT HE SAID ABOUT TOVIK IS TRUE?
IT'S POSSIBLE. HE ALWAYS OBEYED HIS FATHER. HE MIGHT GO TO HIM FIRST.
BUT WHY WOULD HIS FATHER KEEP HIM FROM TELLING THE POLICE?! IT MAKES NO SENSE!

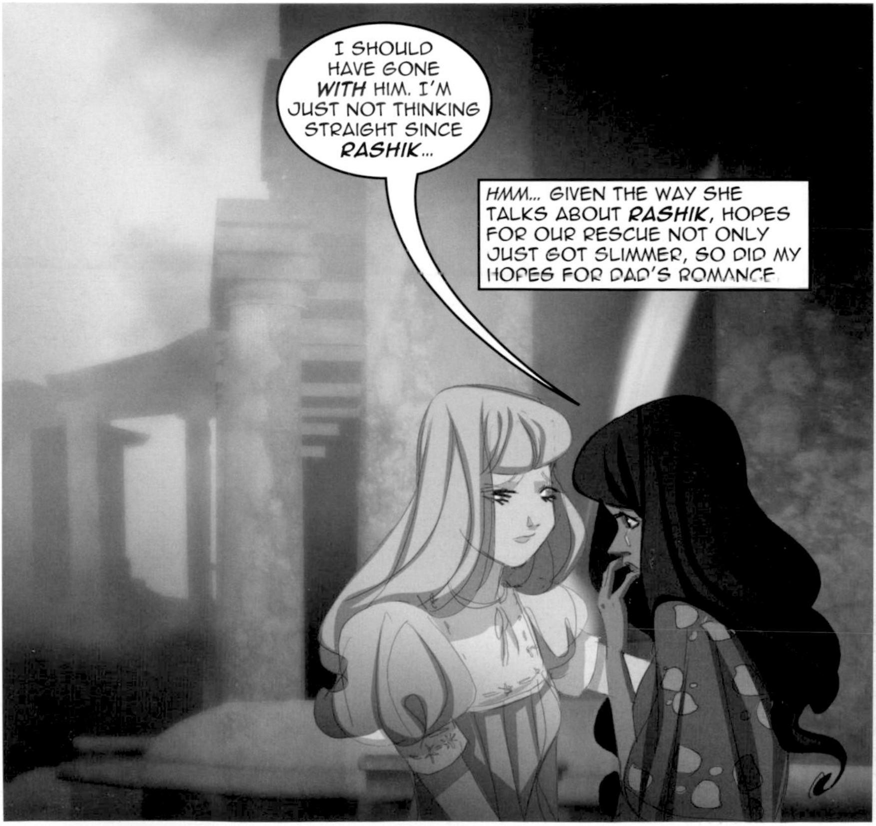
I SHOULD HAVE GONE WITH HIM. I'M JUST NOT THINKING STRAIGHT SINCE RASHIK...
HMM... GIVEN THE WAY SHE TALKS ABOUT RASHIK, HOPES FOR OUR RESCUE NOT ONLY JUST GOT SLIMMER, SO DID MY HOPES FOR DAD'S ROMANCE.

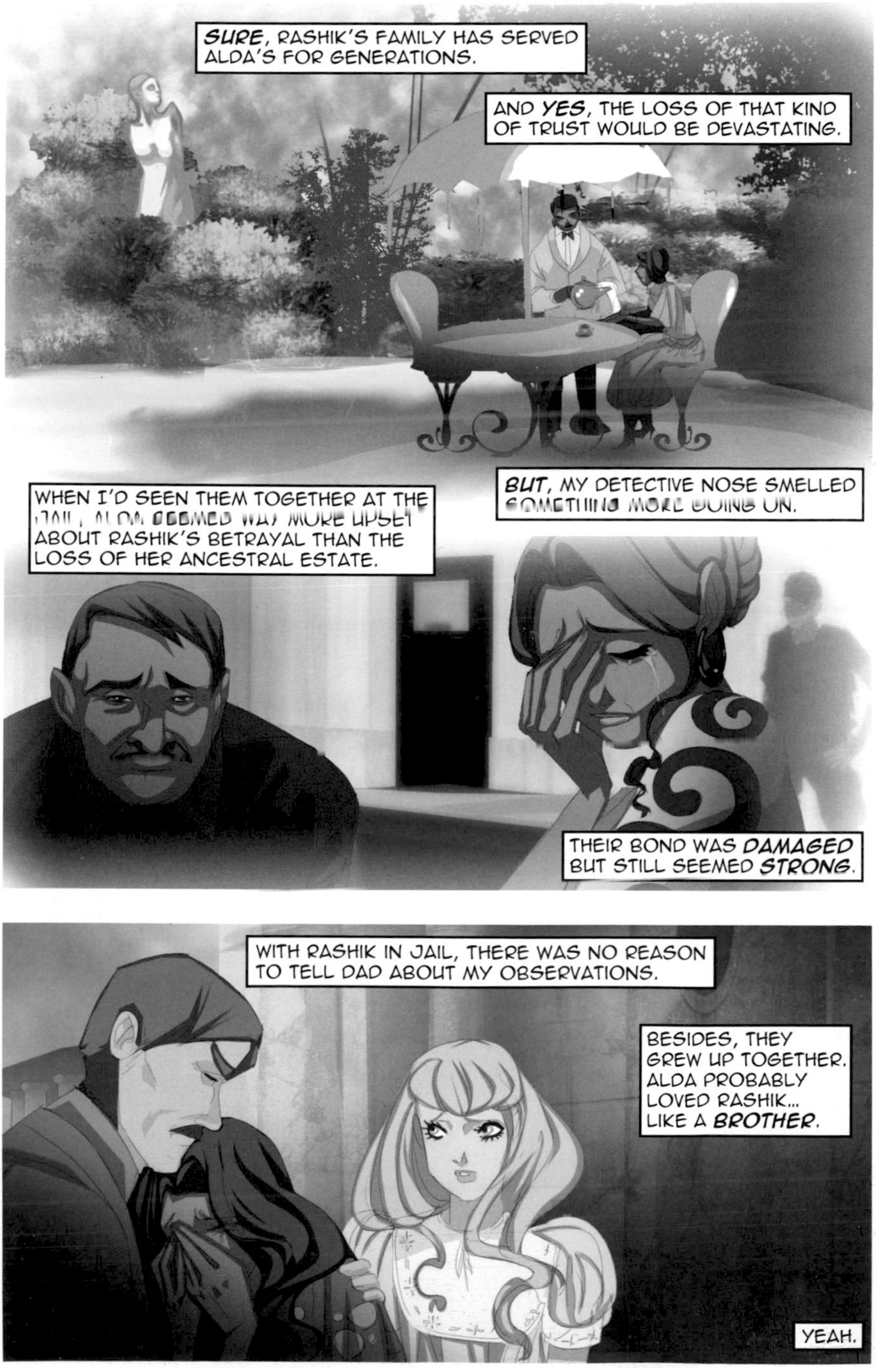
SURE, RASHIK'S FAMILY HAS SERVED ALDA'S FOR GENERATIONS.
AND YES, THE LOSS OF THAT KIND OF TRUST WOULD BE DEVASTATING.
WHEN I'D SEEN THEM TOGETHER AT THE JAIL, ALDA SEEMED WAY MORE UPSET ABOUT RASHIK'S BETRAYAL THAN THE LOSS OF HER ANCESTRAL ESTATE.
BUT, MY DETECTIVE NOSE SMELLED SOMETHING MORE GOING ON.
THEIR BOND WAS DAMAGED BUT STILL SEEMED STRONG.
WITH RASHIK IN JAIL, THERE WAS NO REASON TO TELL DAD ABOUT MY OBSERVATIONS.
BESIDES, THEY GREW UP TOGETHER. ALDA PROBABLY LOVED RASHIK... LIKE A BROTHER.
YEAH.

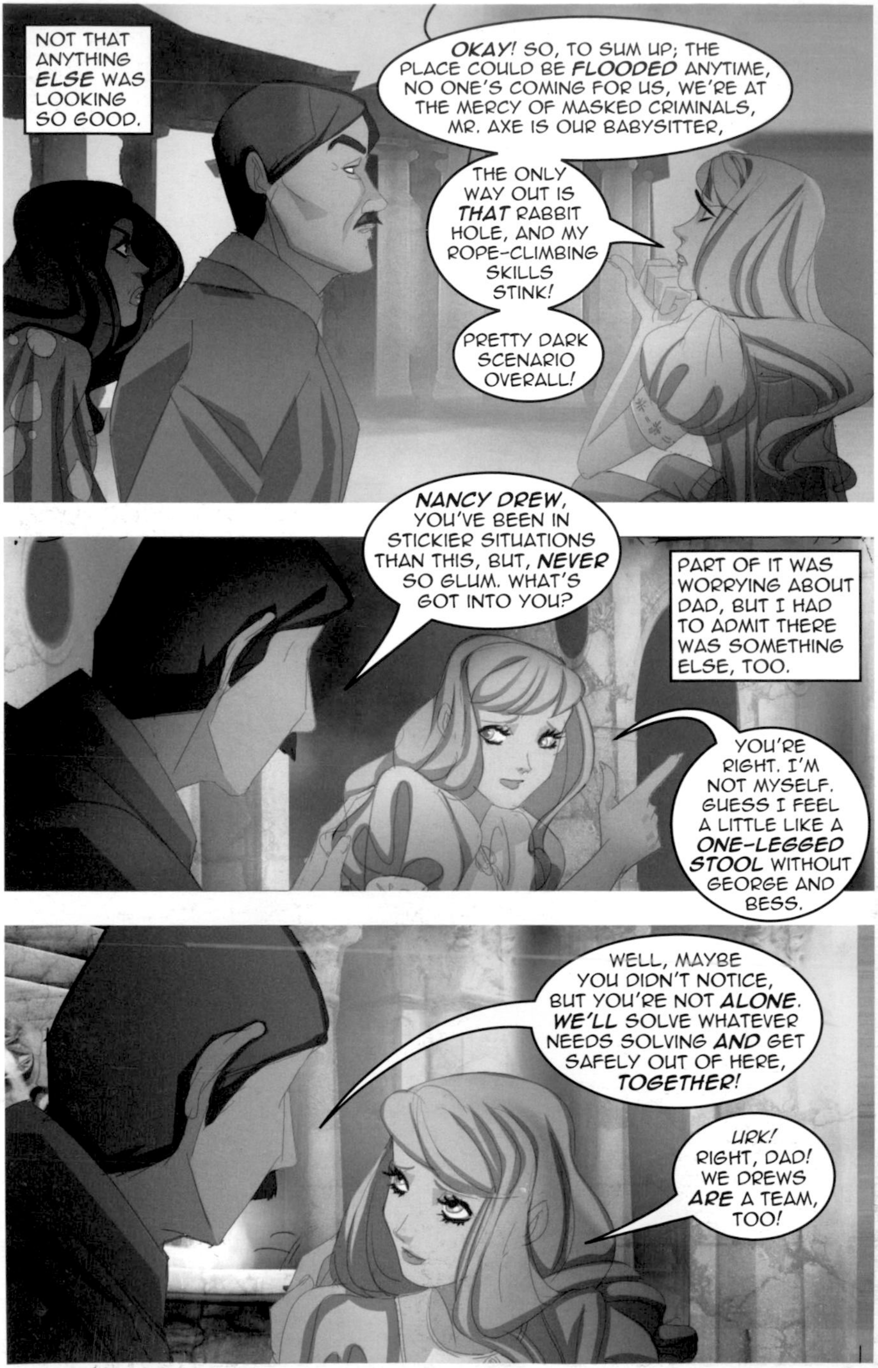

NOT THAT ANYTHING ELSE WAS LOOKING SO GOOD.
OKAY! SO, TO SUM UP; THE PLACE COULD BE FLOODED ANYTIME, NO ONE'S COMING FOR US, WE'RE AT THE MERCY OF MASKED CRIMINALS, MR. AXE IS OUR BABYSITTER,
THE ONLY WAY OUT IS THAT RABBIT HOLE, AND MY ROPE-CLIMBING SKILLS STINK!
PRETTY DARK SCENARIO OVERALL!
NANCY DREW, YOU'VE BEEN IN STICKIER SITUATIONS THAN THIS, BUT, NEVER SO GLUM. WHAT'S GOT INTO YOU?
PART OF IT WAS WORRYING ABOUT DAD, BUT I HAD TO ADMIT THERE WAS SOMETHING ELSE, TOO.
YOU'RE RIGHT. I'M NOT MYSELF. GUESS I FEEL A LITTLE LIKE A ONE-LEGGED STOOL WITHOUT GEORGE AND BESS.
WELL, MAYBE YOU DIDN'T NOTICE, BUT YOU'RE NOT ALONE. WE'LL SOLVE WHATEVER NEEDS SOLVING AND GET SAFELY OUT OF HERE, TOGETHER!
URK! RIGHT, DAD! WE DREWS ARE A TEAM, TOO!

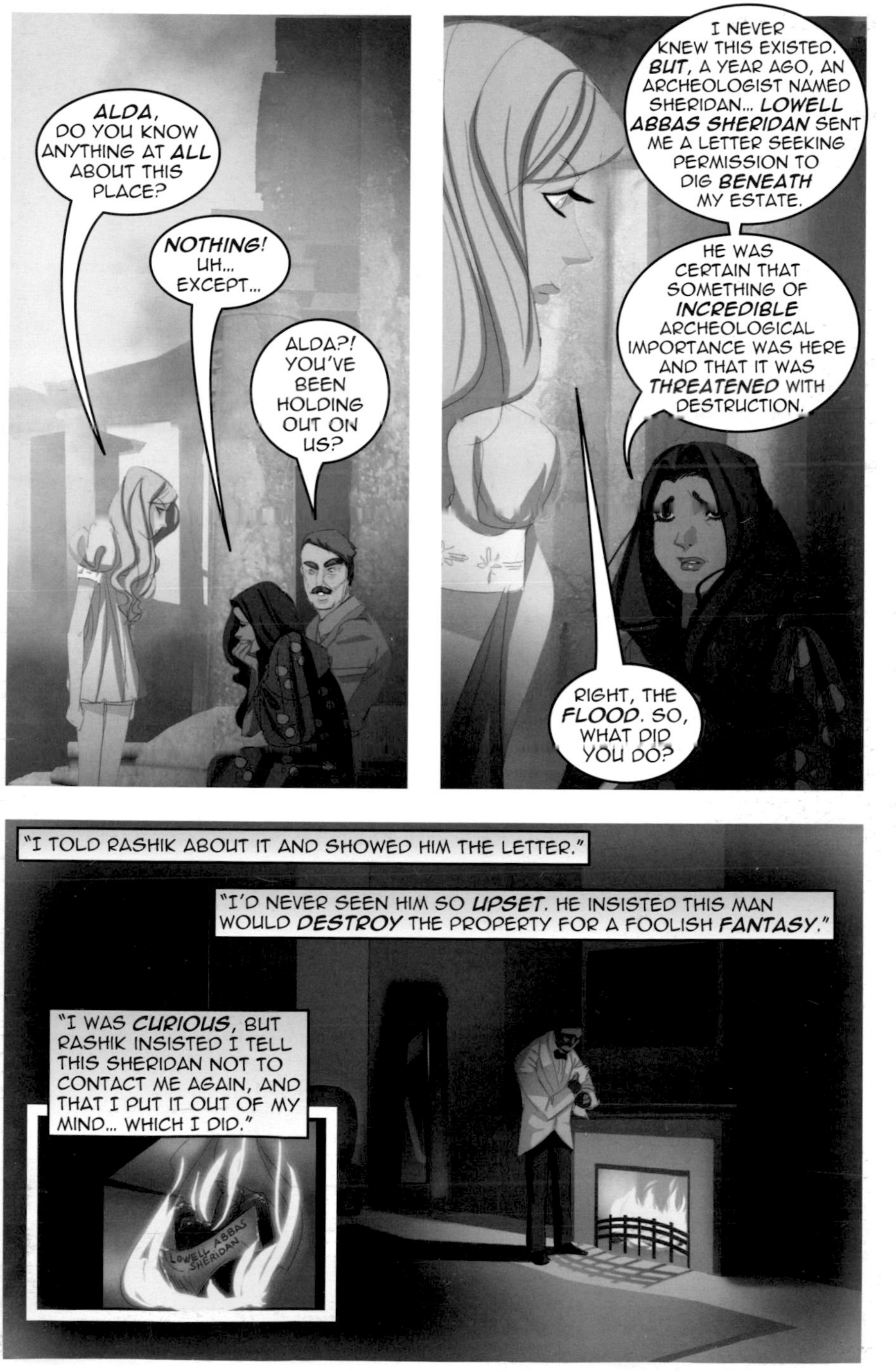

ALDA, DO YOU KNOW ANYTHING AT ALL ABOUT THIS PLACE?
NOTHING! UH... EXCEPT...
ALDA?! YOU'VE BEEN HOLDING OUT ON US?
I NEVER KNEW THIS EXISTED. BUT, A YEAR AGO, AN ARCHEOLOGIST NAMED SHERIDAN... LOWELL ABBAS SHERIDAN SENT ME A LETTER SEEKING PERMISSION TO DIG BENEATH MY ESTATE.
HE WAS CERTAIN THAT SOMETHING OF INCREDIBLE ARCHEOLOGICAL IMPORTANCE WAS HERE AND THAT IT WAS THREATENED WITH DESTRUCTION.
RIGHT, THE FLOOD. SO, WHAT DID YOU DO?
"I TOLD RASHIK ABOUT IT AND SHOWED HIM THE LETTER."
"I'D NEVER SEEN HIM SO UPSET. HE INSISTED THIS MAN WOULD DESTROY THE PROPERTY FOR A FOOLISH FANTASY."
"I WAS CURIOUS, BUT RASHIK INSISTED I TELL THIS SHERIDAN NOT TO CONTACT ME AGAIN, AND THAT I PUT IT OUT OF MY MIND... WHICH I DID."
LOWELL ABBAS SHERIDAN

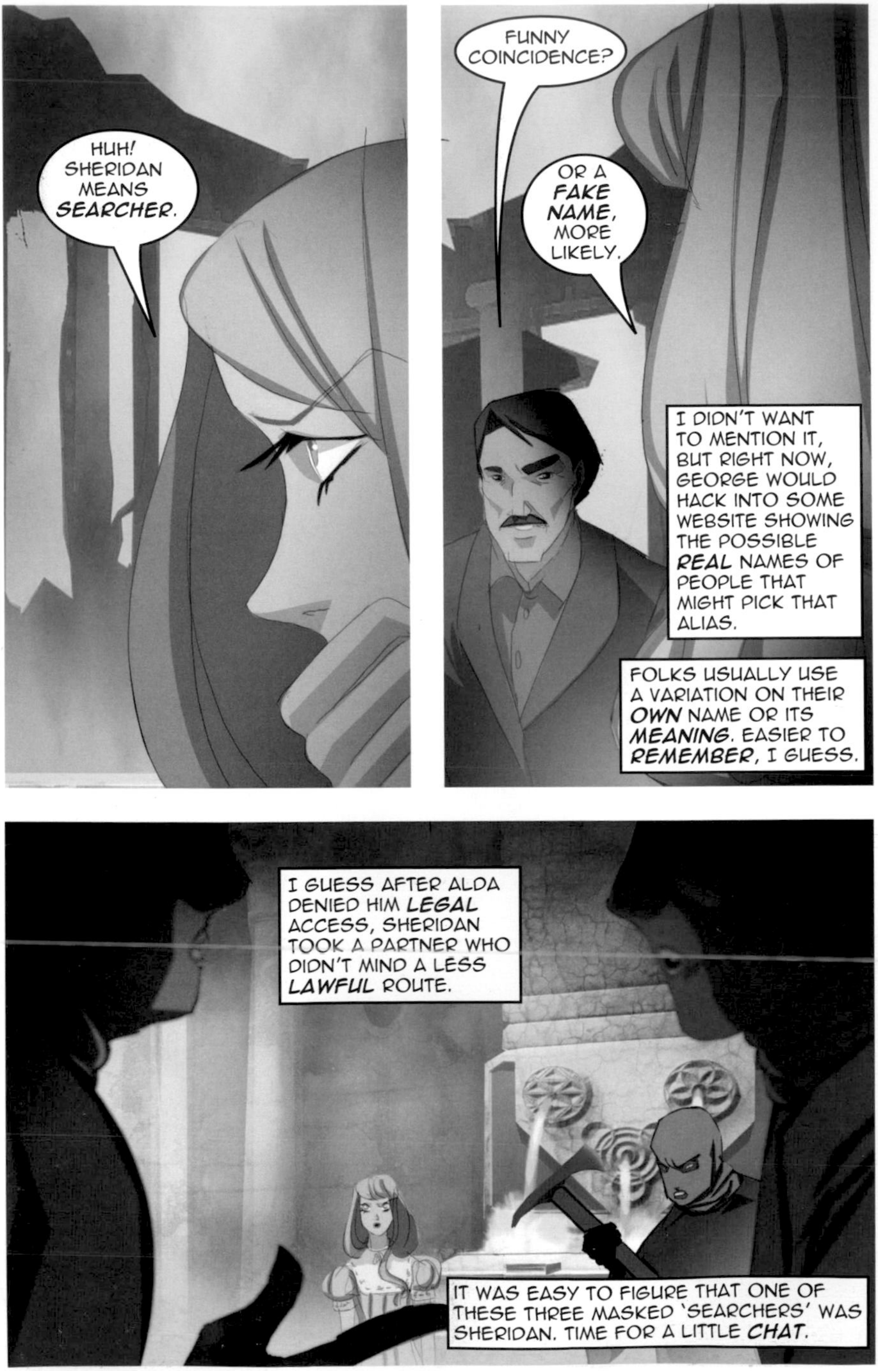
HUH! SHERIDAN MEANS SEARCHER.
FUNNY COINCIDENCE?
OR A FAKE NAME, MORE LIKELY.
I DIDN'T WANT TO MENTION IT, BUT RIGHT NOW, GEORGE WOULD HACK INTO SOME WEBSITE SHOWING THE POSSIBLE REAL NAMES OF PEOPLE THAT MIGHT PICK THAT ALIAS.
FOLKS USUALLY USE A VARIATION ON THEIR OWN NAME OR ITS MEANING. EASIER TO REMEMBER, I GUESS.
I GUESS AFTER ALDA DENIED HIM LEGAL ACCESS, SHERIDAN TOOK A PARTNER WHO DIDN'T MIND A LESS LAWFUL ROUTE.
IT WAS EASY TO FIGURE THAT ONE OF THESE THREE MASKED 'SEARCHERS' WAS SHERIDAN. TIME FOR A LITTLE CHAT.

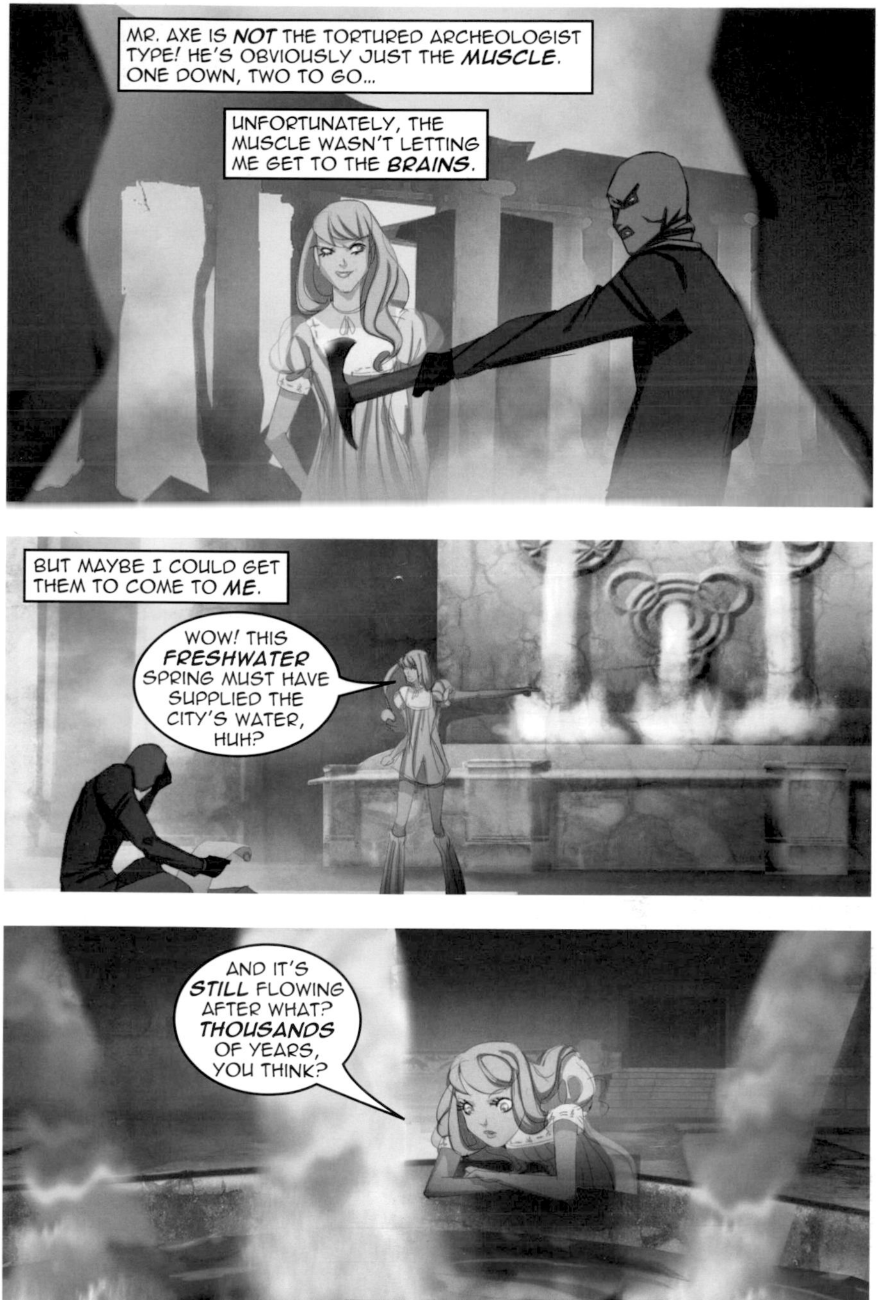
MR. AXE IS NOT THE TORTURED ARCHEOLOGIST TYPE! HE'S OBVIOUSLY JUST THE MUSCLE. ONE DOWN, TWO TO GO...
UNFORTUNATELY, THE MUSCLE WASN'T LETTING ME GET TO THE BRAINS.
BUT MAYBE I COULD GET THEM TO COME TO ME.
WOW! THIS FRESHWATER SPRING MUST HAVE SUPPLIED THE CITY'S WATER, HUH?
AND IT'S STILL FLOWING AFTER WHAT? THOUSANDS OF YEARS, YOU THINK?
CURIOSITY ALWAYS ATTRACTS MORE CURIOSITY OR A TEACHER. EITHER WAY, I HAD HIS ATTENTION.

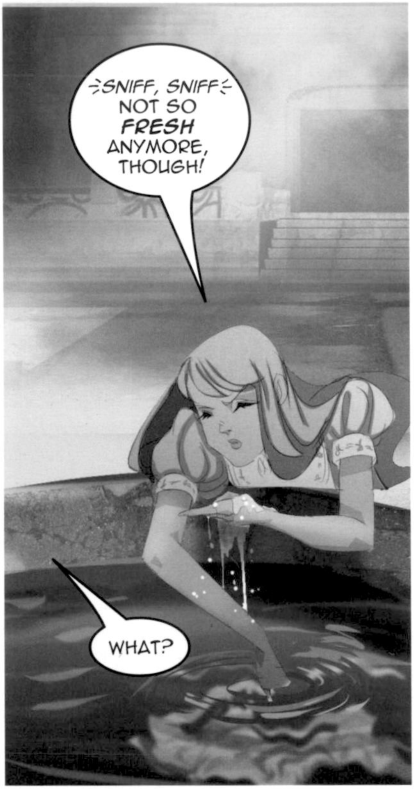

SNIFF, SNIFF NOT SO FRESH ANYMORE, THOUGH!
WHAT?

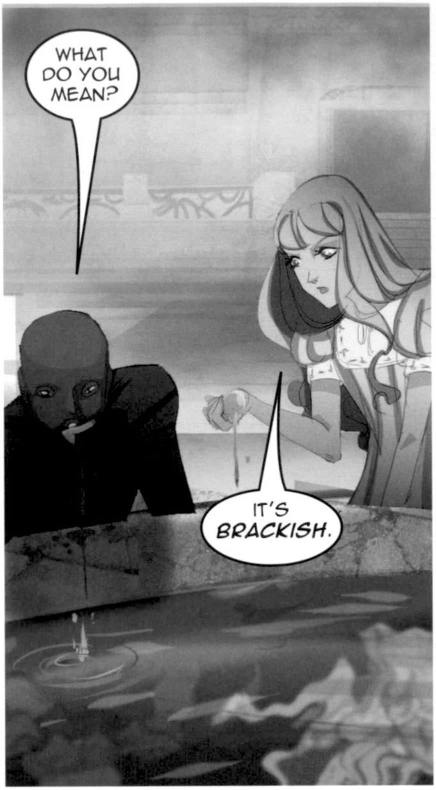

WHAT DO YOU MEAN?
IT'S BRACKISH.

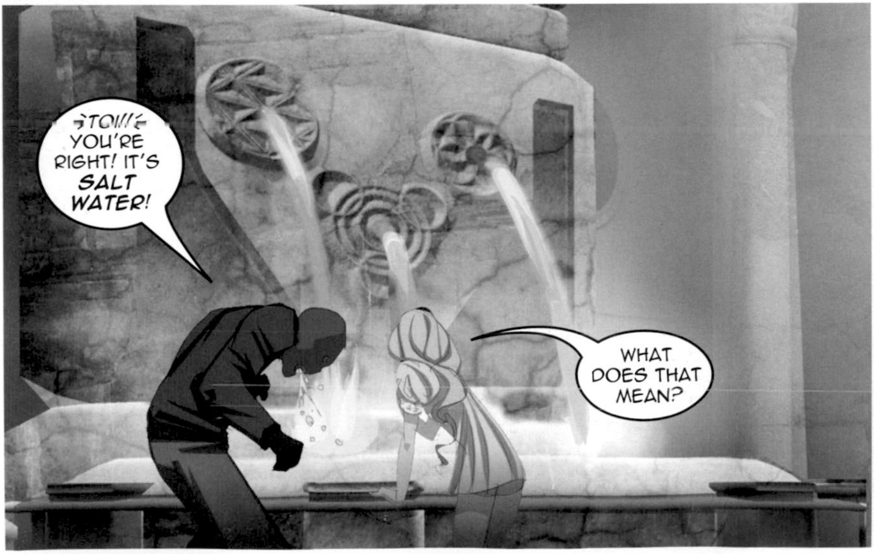

TOI!! YOU'RE RIGHT! IT'S SALT WATER!
WHAT DOES THAT MEAN?

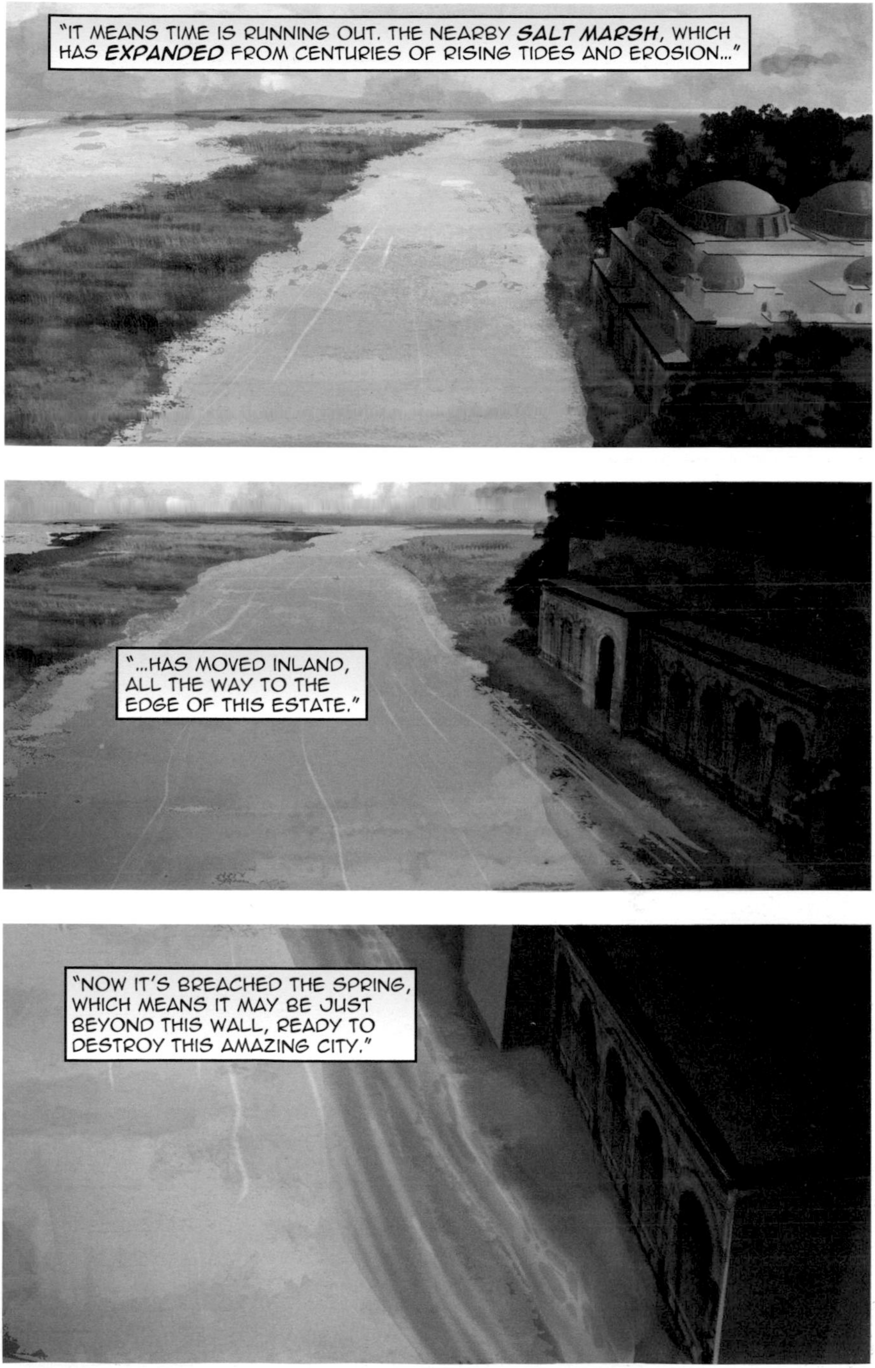
"IT MEANS TIME IS RUNNING OUT. THE NEARBY SALT MARSH, WHICH HAS EXPANDED FROM CENTURIES OF RISING TIDES AND EROSION..."
"...HAS MOVED INLAND, ALL THE WAY TO THE EDGE OF THIS ESTATE."
"NOW IT'S BREACHED THE SPRING, WHICH MEANS IT MAY BE JUST BEYOND THIS WALL, READY TO DESTROY THIS AMAZING CITY."

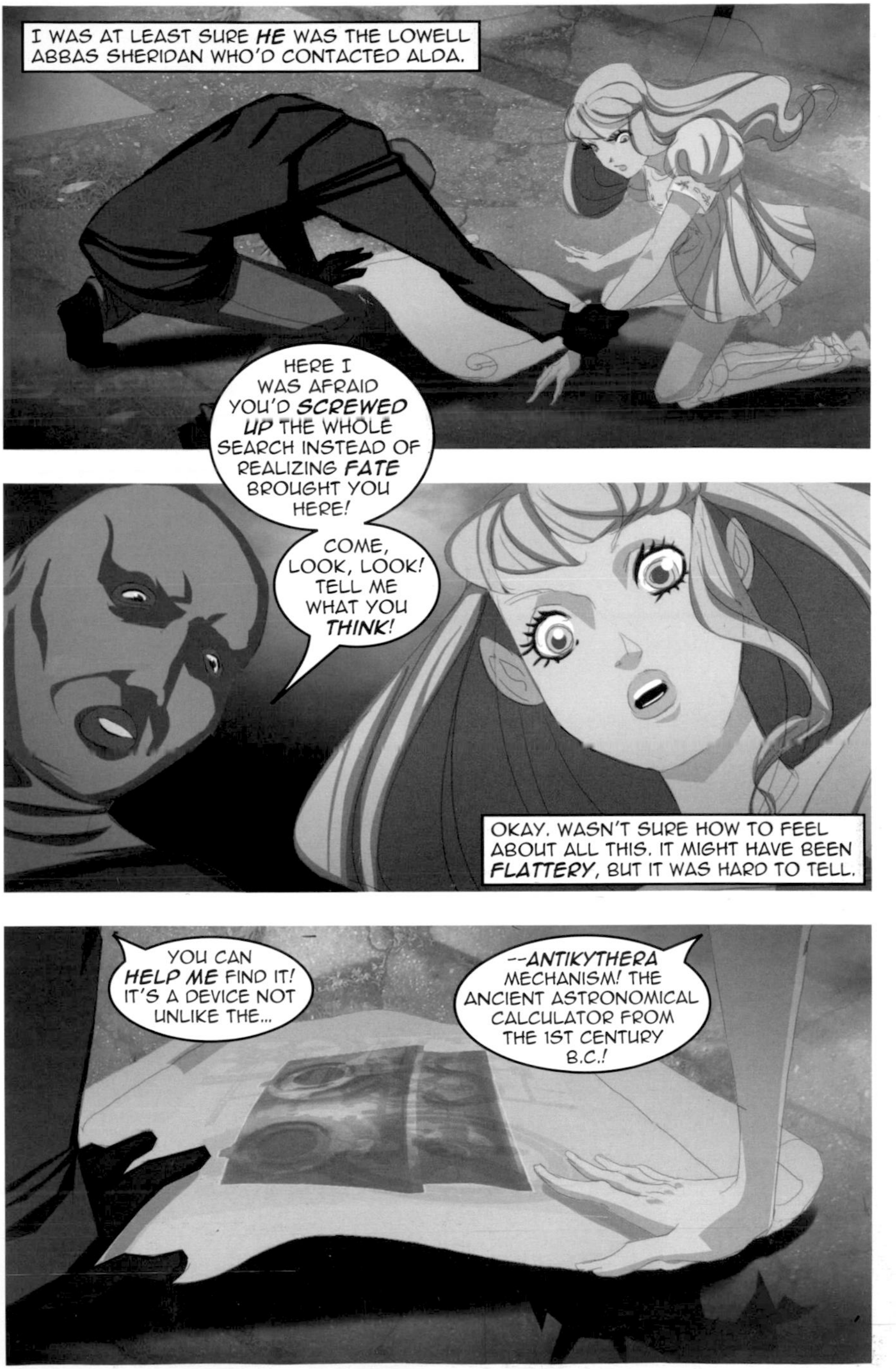
I WAS AT LEAST SURE **HE** WAS THE LOWELL ABBAS SHERIDAN WHO'D CONTACTED ALDA.
HERE I WAS AFRAID YOU'D **SCREWED UP** THE WHOLE SEARCH INSTEAD OF REALIZING **FATE** BROUGHT YOU HERE!
COME, LOOK, LOOK! TELL ME WHAT YOU **THINK**!
OKAY. WASN'T SURE HOW TO FEEL ABOUT ALL THIS. IT MIGHT HAVE BEEN **FLATTERY**, BUT IT WAS HARD TO TELL.
YOU CAN **HELP ME** FIND IT! IT'S A DEVICE NOT UNLIKE THE...
--**ANTIKYTHERA** MECHANISM! THE ANCIENT ASTRONOMICAL CALCULATOR FROM THE 1ST CENTURY B.C.!

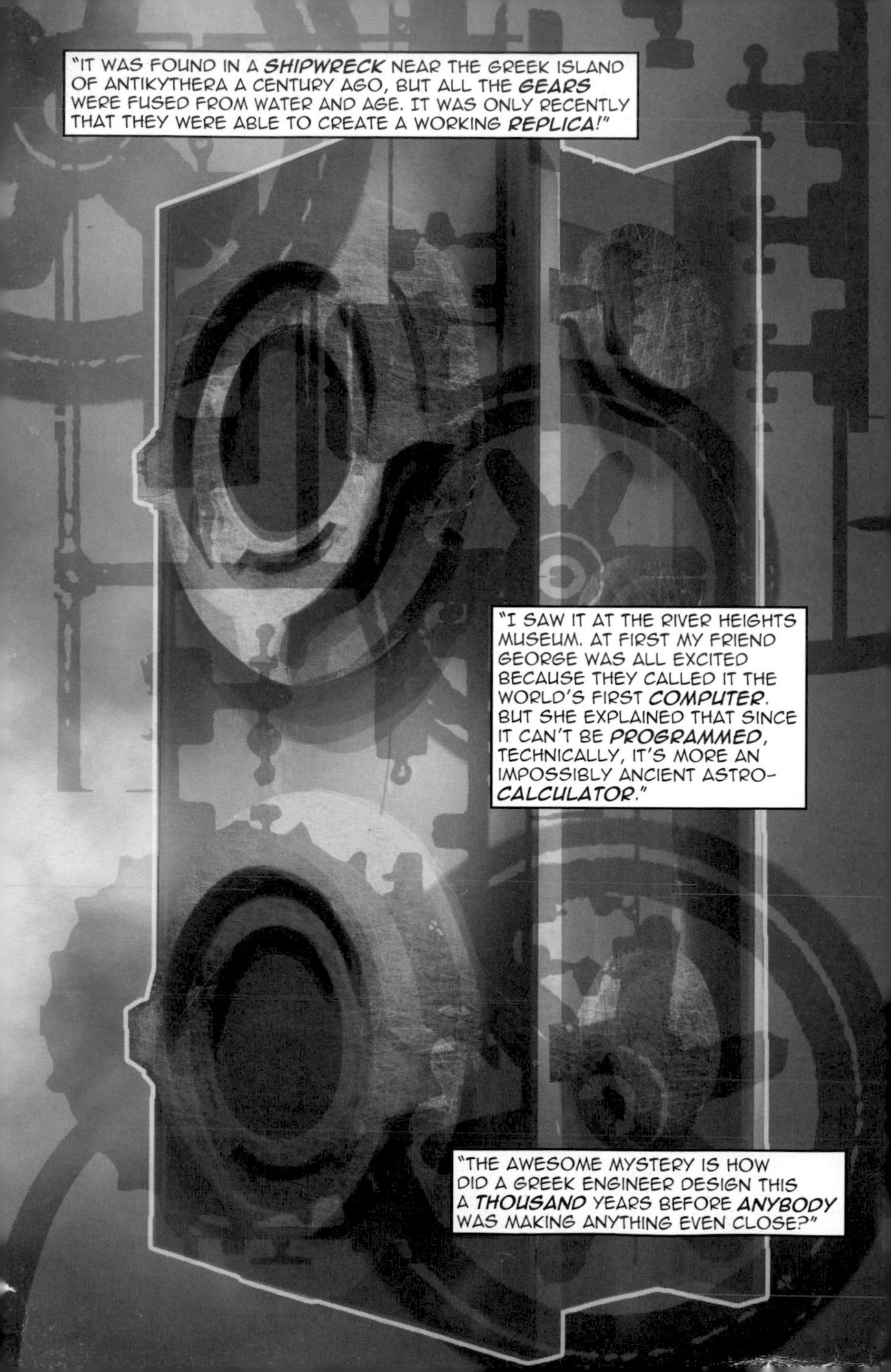
"IT WAS FOUND IN A SHIPWRECK NEAR THE GREEK ISLAND OF ANTIKYTHERA A CENTURY AGO, BUT ALL THE GEARS WERE FUSED FROM WATER AND AGE. IT WAS ONLY RECENTLY THAT THEY WERE ABLE TO CREATE A WORKING REPLICA!"
"I SAW IT AT THE RIVER HEIGHTS MUSEUM. AT FIRST MY FRIEND GEORGE WAS ALL EXCITED BECAUSE THEY CALLED IT THE WORLD'S FIRST COMPUTER. BUT SHE EXPLAINED THAT SINCE IT CAN'T BE PROGRAMMED, TECHNICALLY, IT'S MORE AN IMPOSSIBLY ANCIENT ASTRO-CALCULATOR."
"THE AWESOME MYSTERY IS HOW DID A GREEK ENGINEER DESIGN THIS A THOUSAND YEARS BEFORE ANYBODY WAS MAKING ANYTHING EVEN CLOSE?"

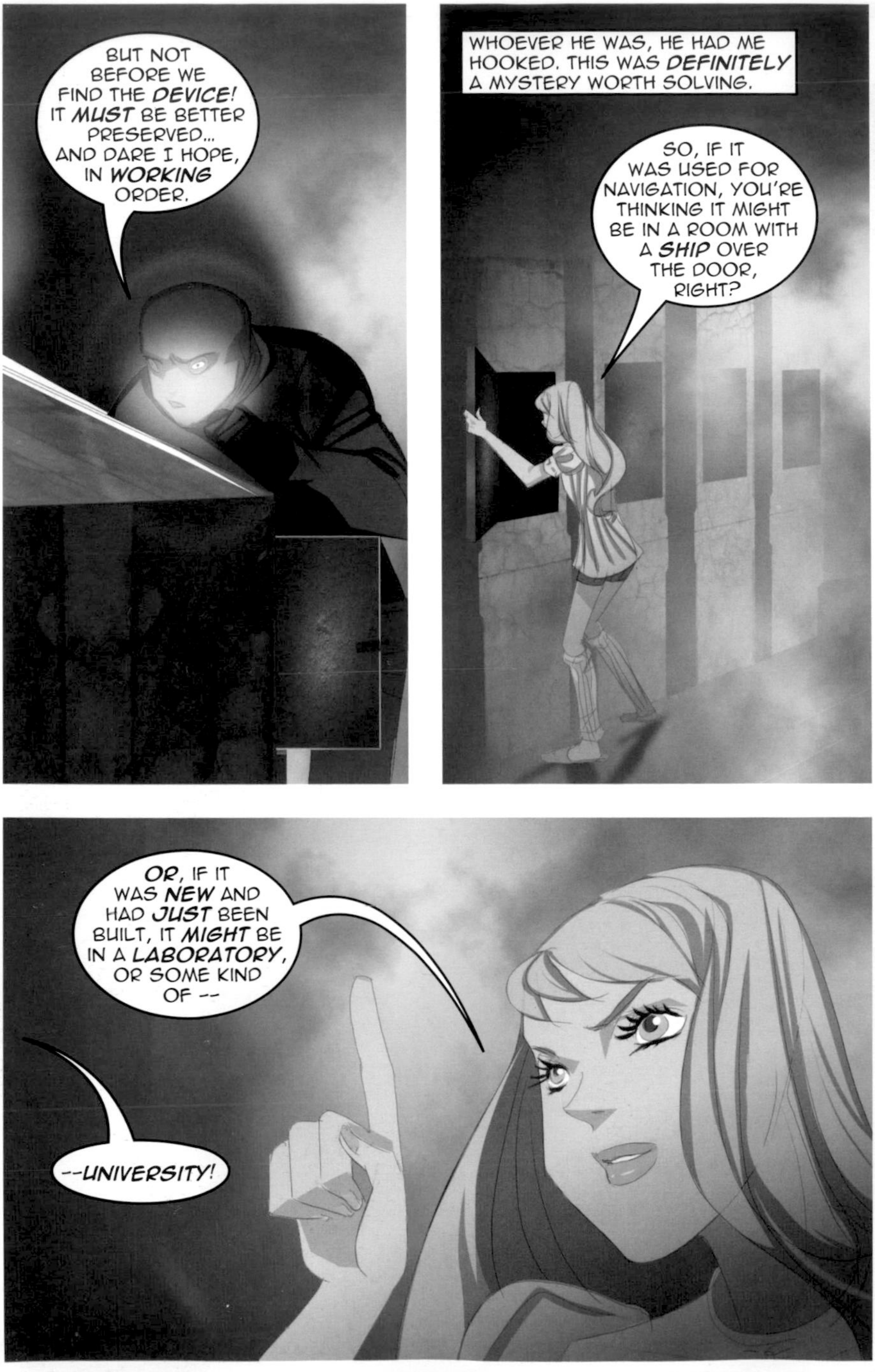
BUT NOT BEFORE WE FIND THE DEVICE! IT MUST BE BETTER PRESERVED... AND DARE I HOPE, IN WORKING ORDER.
WHOEVER HE WAS, HE HAD ME HOOKED. THIS WAS DEFINITELY A MYSTERY WORTH SOLVING.
SO, IF IT WAS USED FOR NAVIGATION, YOU'RE THINKING IT MIGHT BE IN A ROOM WITH A SHIP OVER THE DOOR, RIGHT?
OR, IF IT WAS NEW AND HAD JUST BEEN BUILT, IT MIGHT BE IN A LABORATORY, OR SOME KIND OF --
--UNIVERSITY!

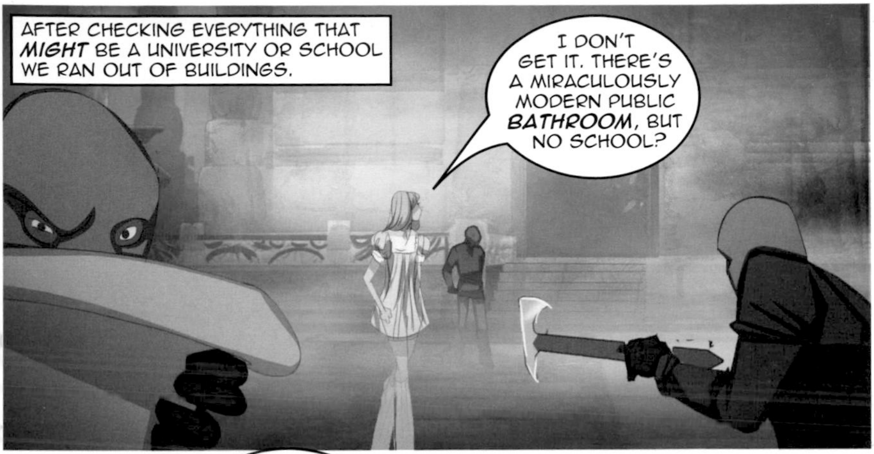
AFTER CHECKING EVERYTHING THAT *MIGHT* BE A UNIVERSITY OR SCHOOL WE RAN OUT OF BUILDINGS.
I DON'T GET IT. THERE'S A MIRACULOUSLY MODERN PUBLIC **BATHROOM**, BUT NO SCHOOL?

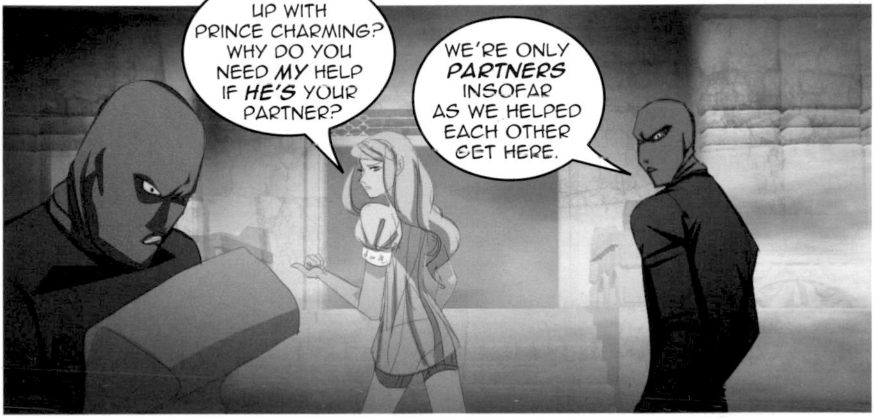
WHAT'S UP WITH PRINCE CHARMING? WHY DO YOU NEED *MY* HELP IF *HE'S* YOUR PARTNER?
WE'RE ONLY **PARTNERS** INSOFAR AS WE HELPED EACH OTHER GET HERE.

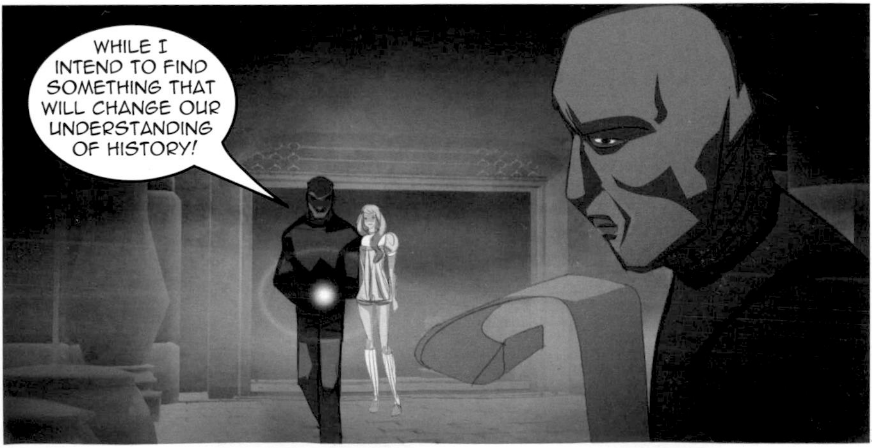
WHILE I INTEND TO FIND SOMETHING THAT WILL CHANGE OUR UNDERSTANDING OF HISTORY!

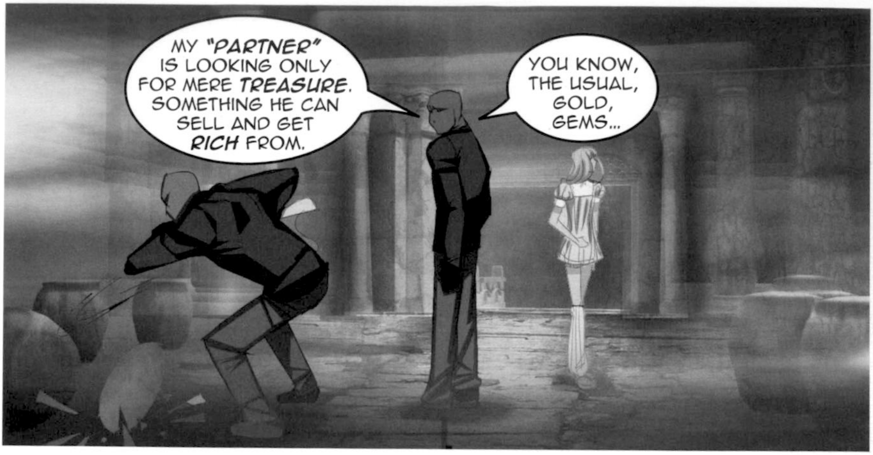
MY "PARTNER" IS LOOKING ONLY FOR MERE TREASURE. SOMETHING HE CAN SELL AND GET RICH FROM.
YOU KNOW, THE USUAL, GOLD, GEMS...

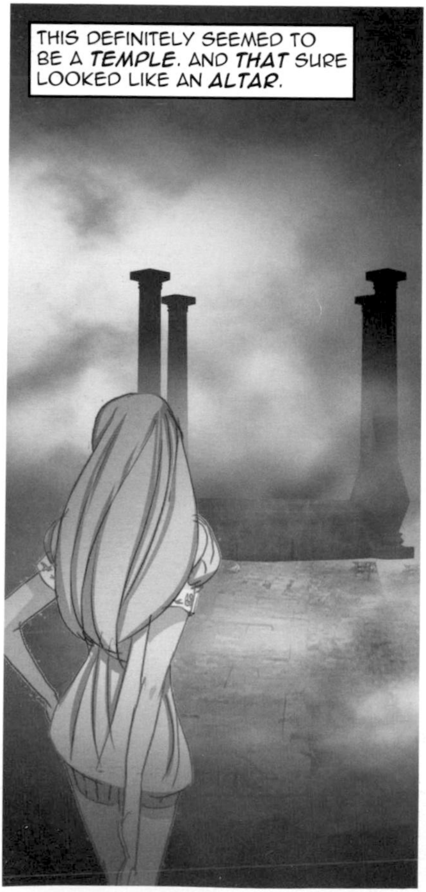
THIS DEFINITELY SEEMED TO BE A TEMPLE. AND THAT SURE LOOKED LIKE AN ALTAR.

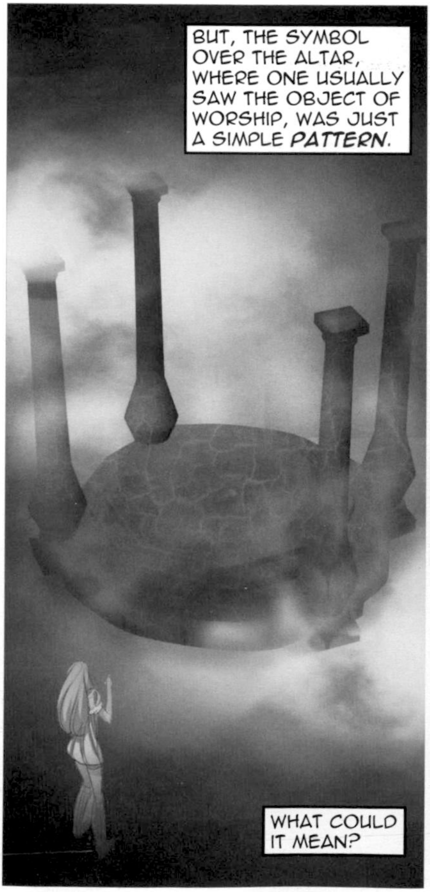
BUT, THE SYMBOL OVER THE ALTAR, WHERE ONE USUALLY SAW THE OBJECT OF WORSHIP, WAS JUST A SIMPLE PATTERN.
WHAT COULD IT MEAN?

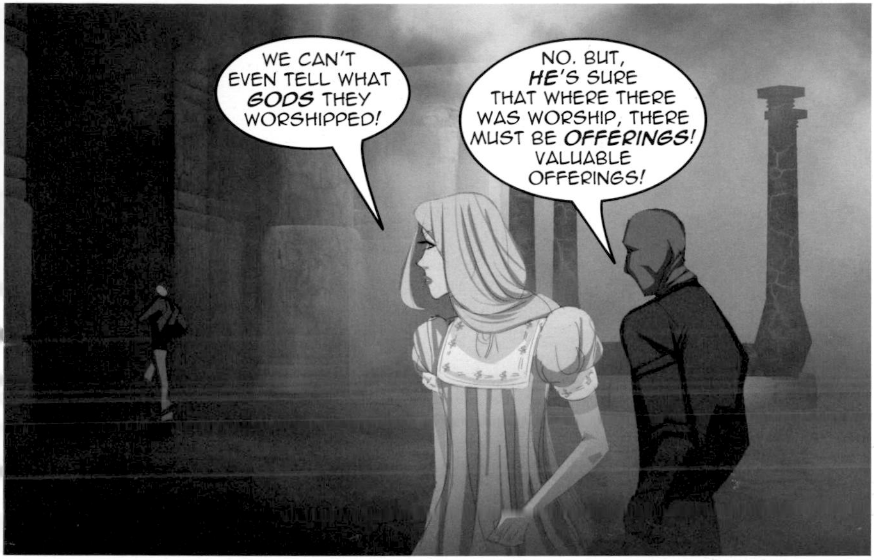
WE CAN'T EVEN TELL WHAT GODS THEY WORSHIPPED!
NO. BUT, HE'S SURE THAT WHERE THERE WAS WORSHIP, THERE MUST BE OFFERINGS! VALUABLE OFFERINGS!

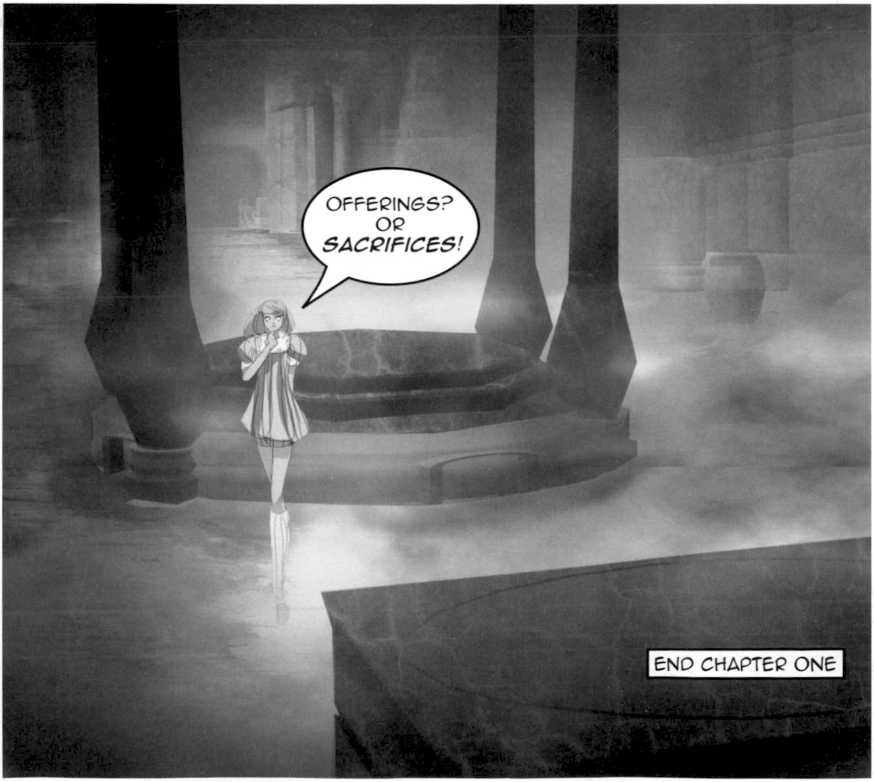
OFFERINGS? OR SACRIFICES!
END CHAPTER ONE

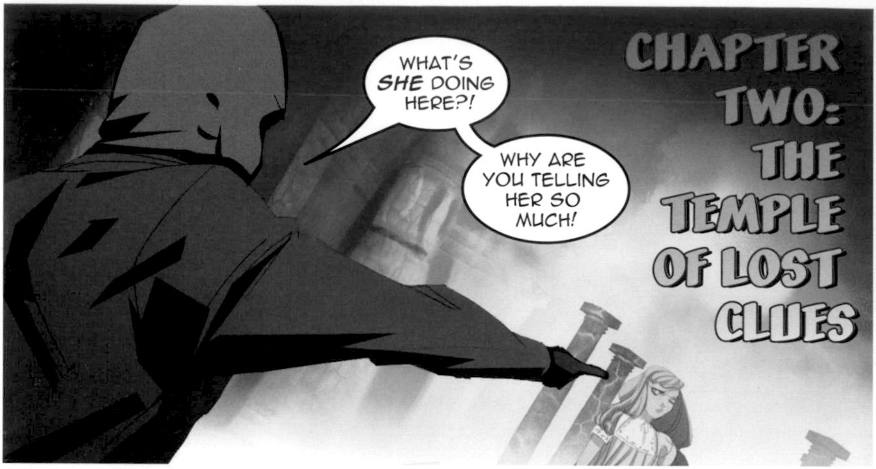
CHAPTER TWO: THE TEMPLE OF LOST CLUES
WHAT'S SHE DOING HERE?!
WHY ARE YOU TELLING HER SO MUCH!

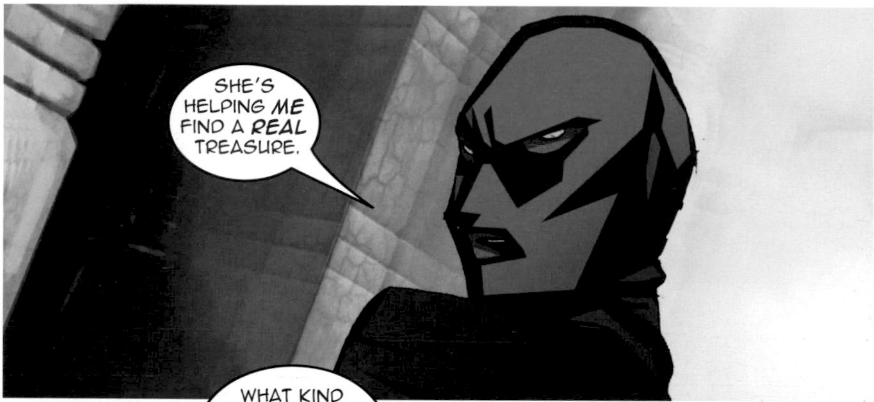
SHE'S HELPING ME FIND A REAL TREASURE.

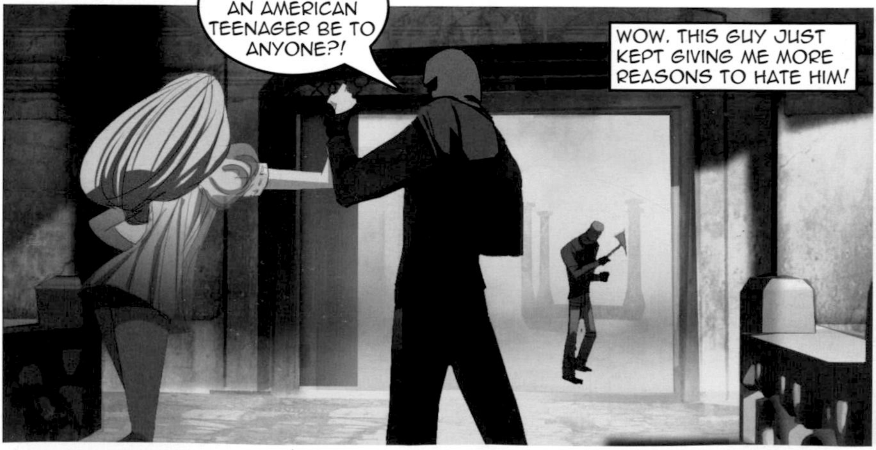
WHAT KIND OF HELP COULD AN AMERICAN TEENAGER BE TO ANYONE?!
WOW. THIS GUY JUST KEPT GIVING ME MORE REASONS TO HATE HIM!

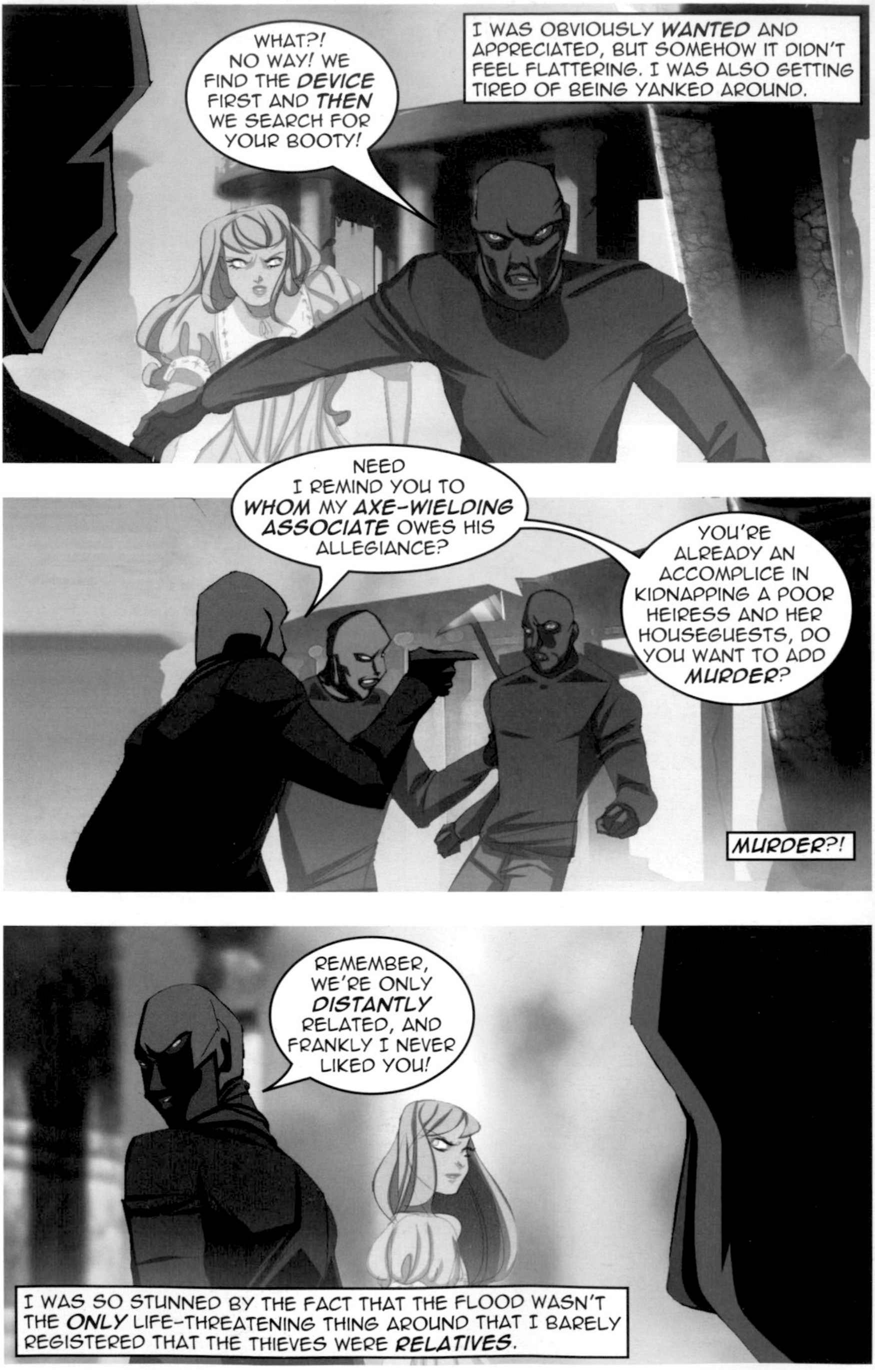
WHAT?! NO WAY! WE FIND THE *DEVICE* FIRST AND *THEN* WE SEARCH FOR YOUR BOOTY!
I WAS OBVIOUSLY *WANTED* AND APPRECIATED, BUT SOMEHOW IT DIDN'T FEEL FLATTERING. I WAS ALSO GETTING TIRED OF BEING YANKED AROUND.
NEED I REMIND YOU TO *WHOM* MY *AXE-WIELDING ASSOCIATE* OWES HIS ALLEGIANCE?
YOU'RE ALREADY AN ACCOMPLICE IN KIDNAPPING A POOR HEIRESS AND HER HOUSEGUESTS, DO YOU WANT TO ADD *MURDER*?
MURDER?!
REMEMBER, WE'RE ONLY *DISTANTLY* RELATED, AND FRANKLY I NEVER LIKED YOU!
I WAS SO STUNNED BY THE FACT THAT THE FLOOD WASN'T THE *ONLY* LIFE-THREATENING THING AROUND THAT I BARELY REGISTERED THAT THE THIEVES WERE *RELATIVES*.

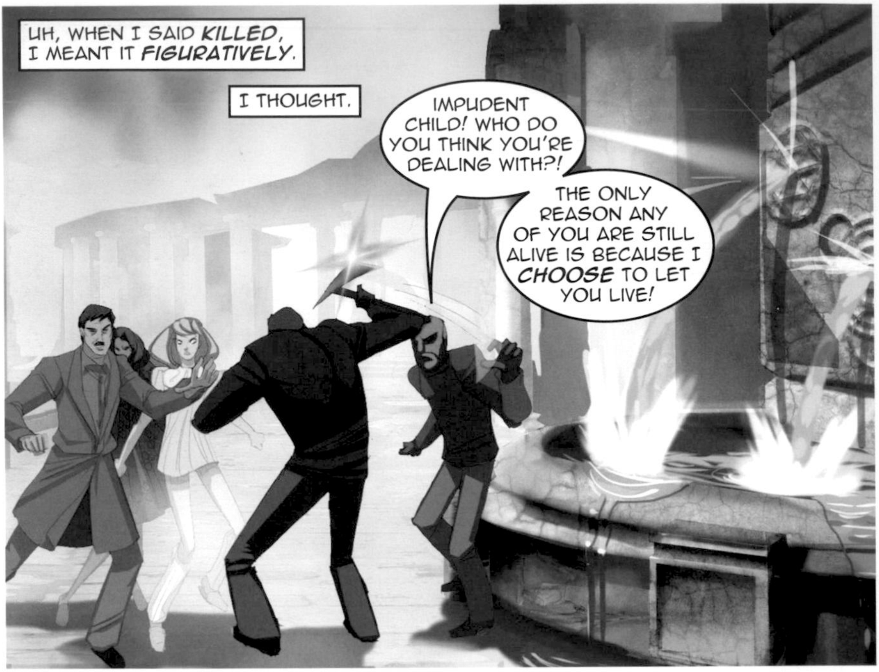
UH, WHEN I SAID KILLED, I MEANT IT FIGURATIVELY.
I THOUGHT.
IMPUDENT CHILD! WHO DO YOU THINK YOU'RE DEALING WITH?!
THE ONLY REASON ANY OF YOU ARE STILL ALIVE IS BECAUSE I CHOOSE TO LET YOU LIVE!

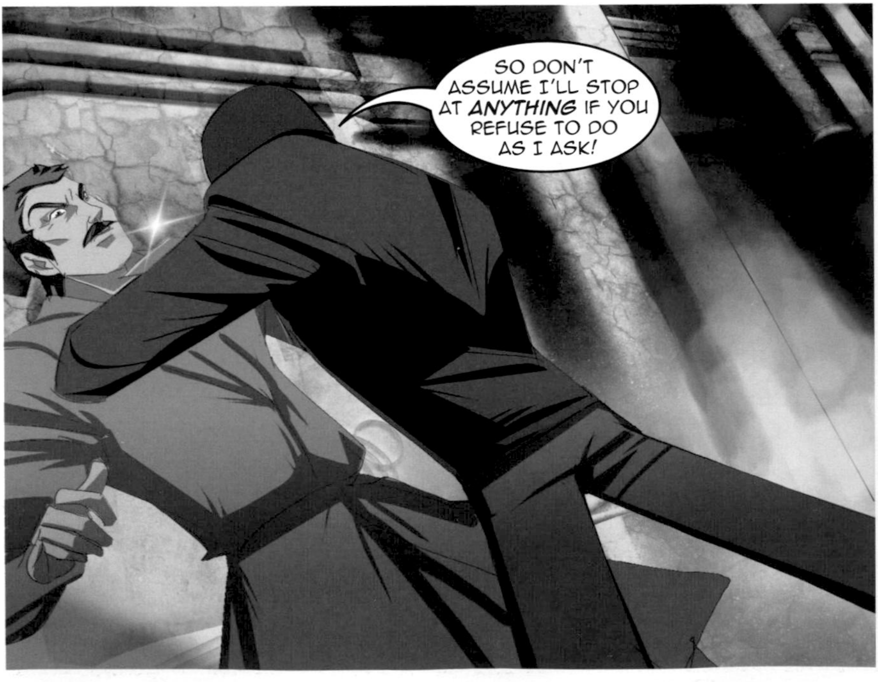
SO DON'T ASSUME I'LL STOP AT ANYTHING IF YOU REFUSE TO DO AS I ASK!

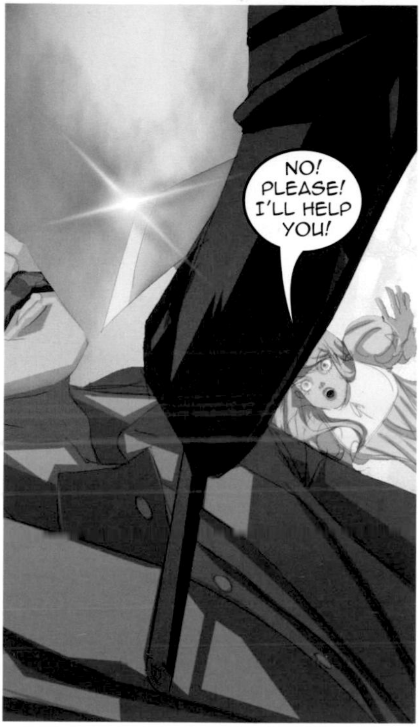
NO! PLEASE! I'LL HELP YOU!

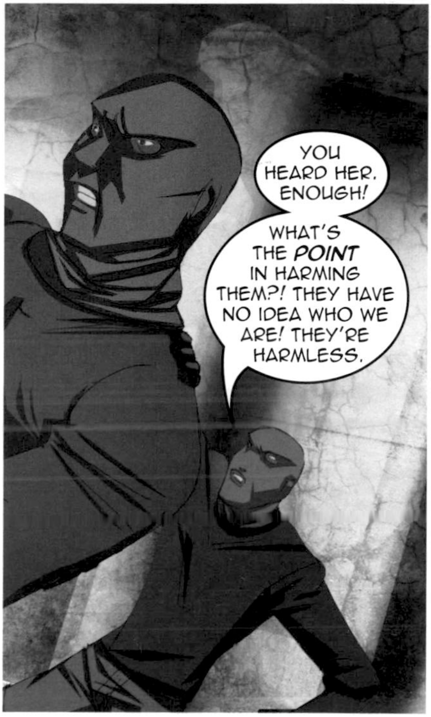
YOU HEARD HER. ENOUGH!
WHAT'S THE POINT IN HARMING THEM?! THEY HAVE NO IDEA WHO WE ARE! THEY'RE HARMLESS.

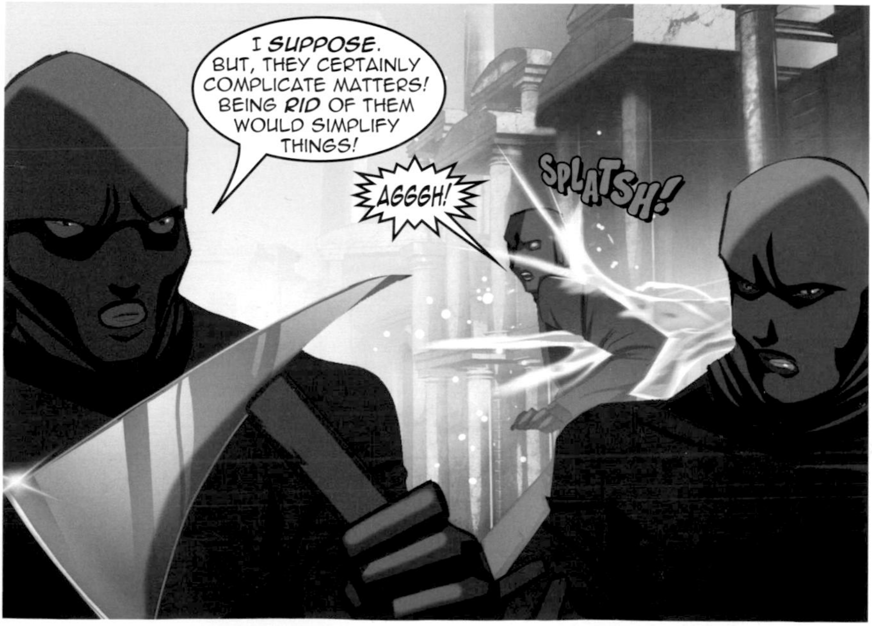
I SUPPOSE. BUT, THEY CERTAINLY COMPLICATE MATTERS! BEING RID OF THEM WOULD SIMPLIFY THINGS!
AGGGH!
SPLATSH!

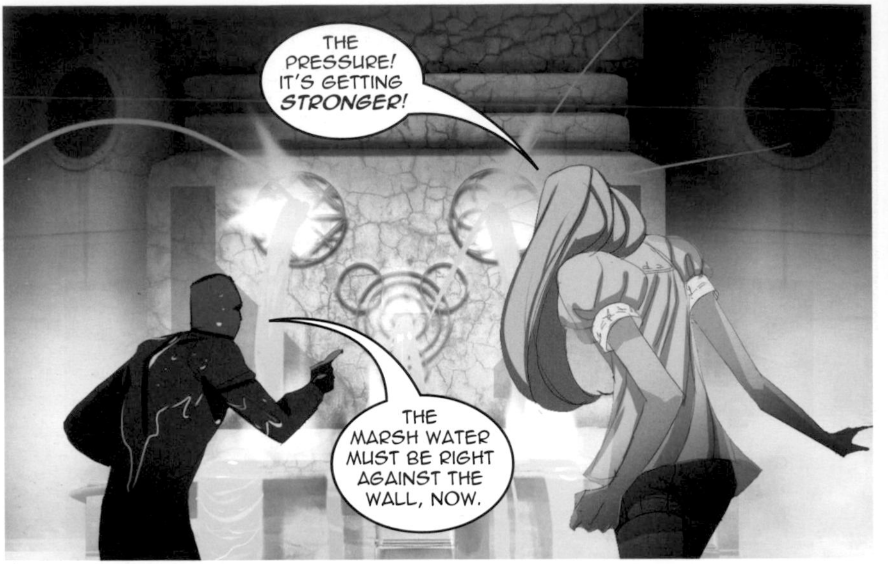
THE PRESSURE! IT'S GETTING STRONGER!
THE MARSH WATER MUST BE RIGHT AGAINST THE WALL, NOW.

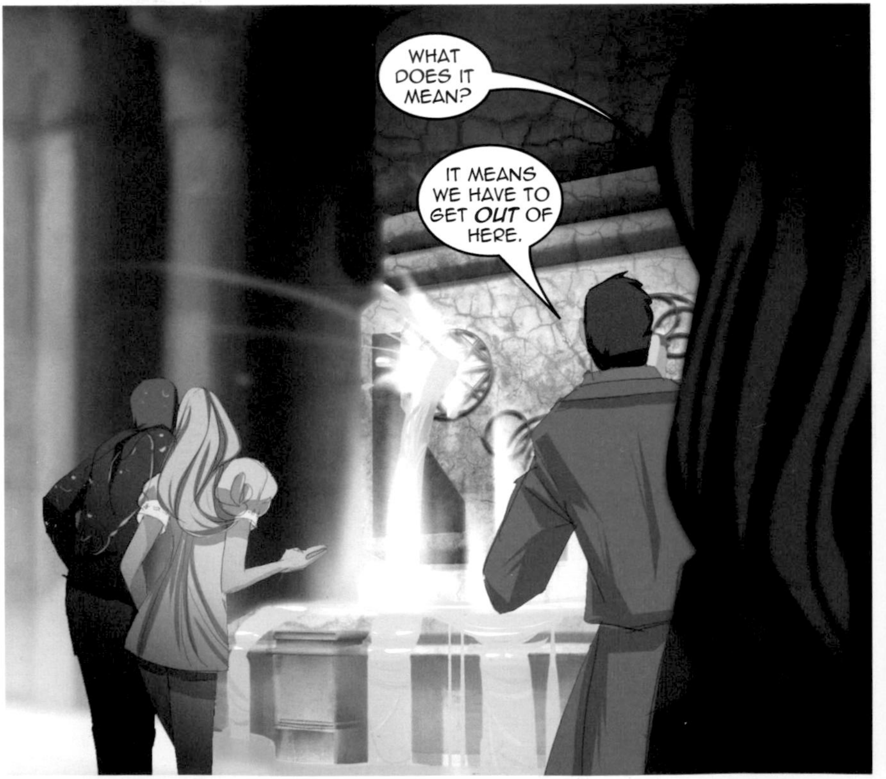
WHAT DOES IT MEAN?
IT MEANS WE HAVE TO GET OUT OF HERE.

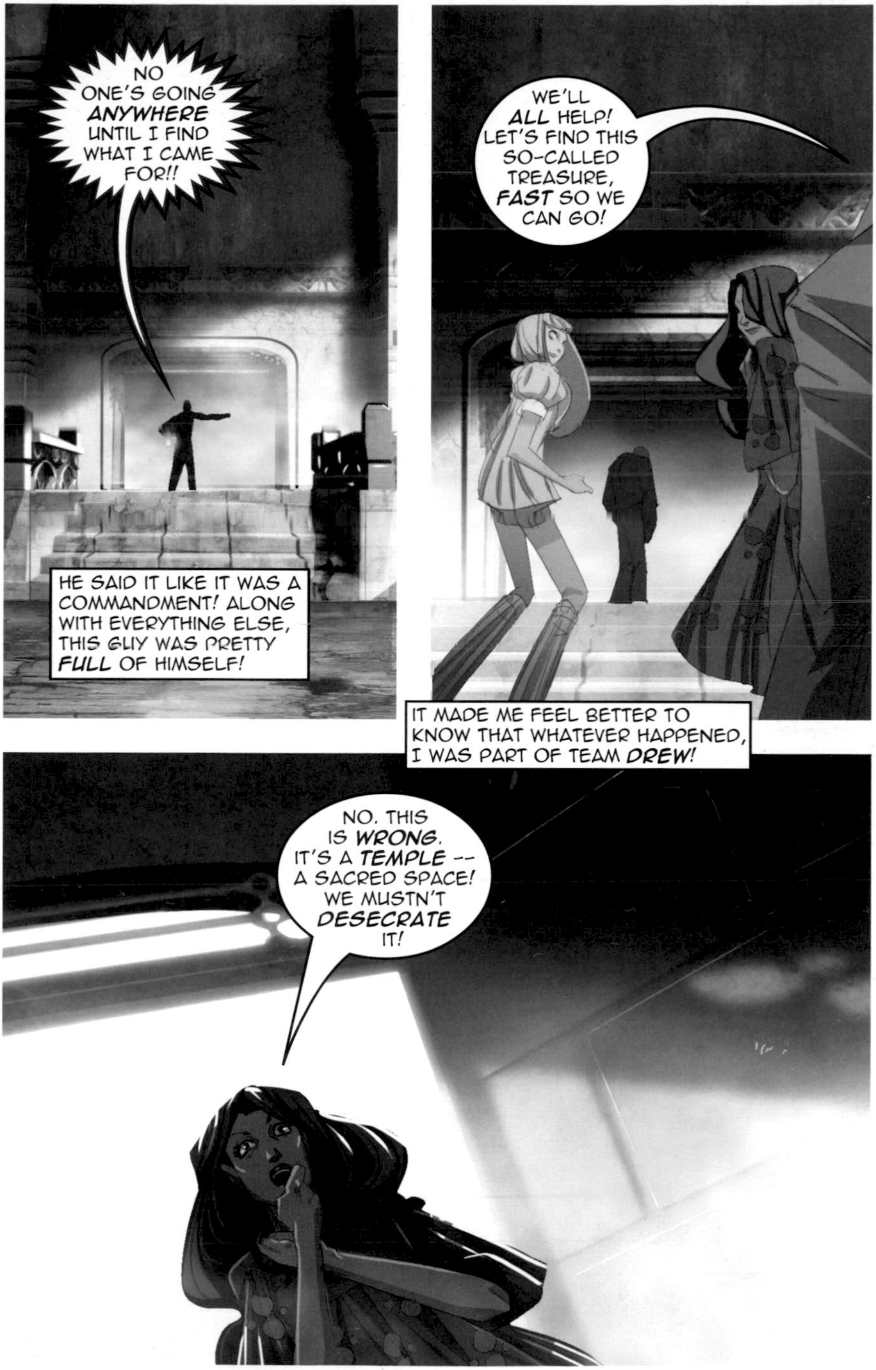

NO ONE'S GOING ANYWHERE UNTIL I FIND WHAT I CAME FOR!!
HE SAID IT LIKE IT WAS A COMMANDMENT! ALONG WITH EVERYTHING ELSE, THIS GUY WAS PRETTY FULL OF HIMSELF!
WE'LL ALL HELP! LET'S FIND THIS SO-CALLED TREASURE, FAST SO WE CAN GO!
IT MADE ME FEEL BETTER TO KNOW THAT WHATEVER HAPPENED, I WAS PART OF TEAM DREW!
NO. THIS IS WRONG. IT'S A TEMPLE -- A SACRED SPACE! WE MUSTN'T DESECRATE IT!

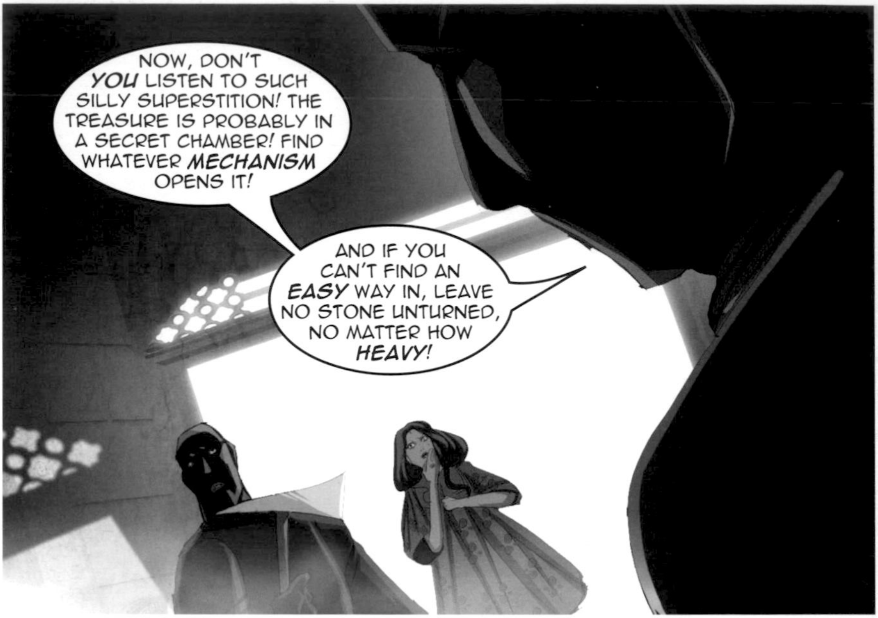
NOW, DON'T *YOU* LISTEN TO SUCH SILLY SUPERSTITION! THE TREASURE IS PROBABLY IN A SECRET CHAMBER! FIND WHATEVER *MECHANISM* OPENS IT!
AND IF YOU CAN'T FIND AN *EASY* WAY IN, LEAVE NO STONE UNTURNED, NO MATTER HOW *HEAVY*!

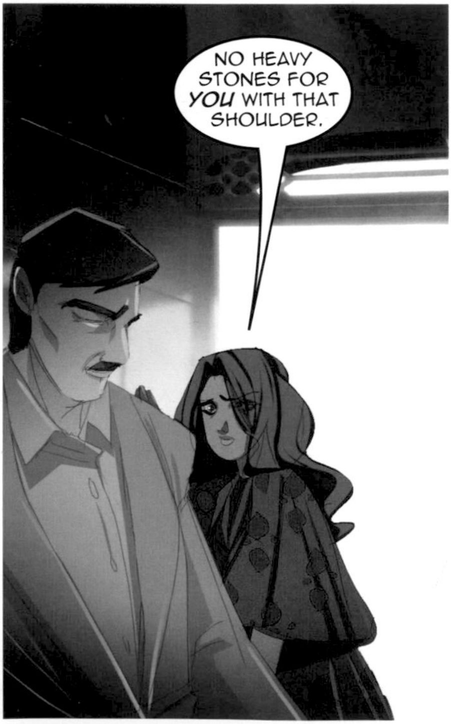
NO HEAVY STONES FOR *YOU* WITH THAT SHOULDER.

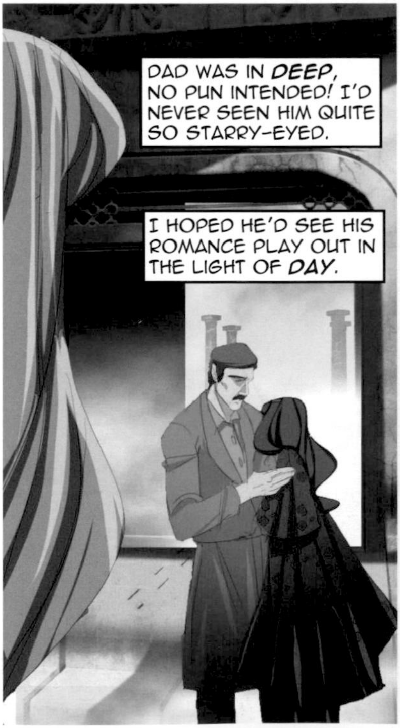
DAD WAS IN *DEEP*, NO PUN INTENDED! I'D NEVER SEEN HIM QUITE SO STARRY-EYED.
I HOPED HE'D SEE HIS ROMANCE PLAY OUT IN THE LIGHT OF *DAY*.

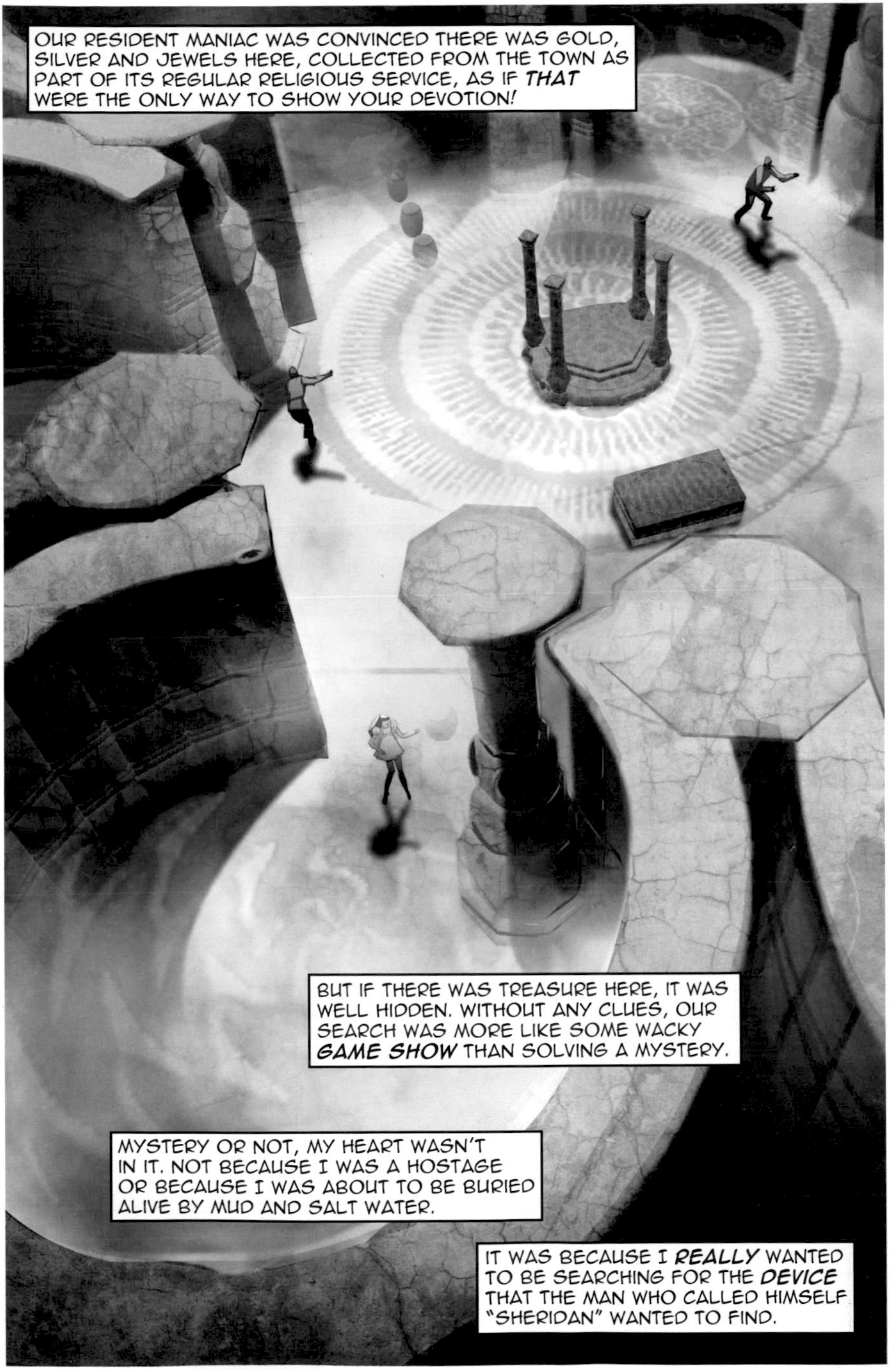
OUR RESIDENT MANIAC WAS CONVINCED THERE WAS GOLD, SILVER AND JEWELS HERE, COLLECTED FROM THE TOWN AS PART OF ITS REGULAR RELIGIOUS SERVICE, AS IF *THAT* WERE THE ONLY WAY TO SHOW YOUR DEVOTION!
BUT IF THERE WAS TREASURE HERE, IT WAS WELL HIDDEN. WITHOUT ANY CLUES, OUR SEARCH WAS MORE LIKE SOME WACKY *GAME SHOW* THAN SOLVING A MYSTERY.
MYSTERY OR NOT, MY HEART WASN'T IN IT. NOT BECAUSE I WAS A HOSTAGE OR BECAUSE I WAS ABOUT TO BE BURIED ALIVE BY MUD AND SALT WATER.
IT WAS BECAUSE I *REALLY* WANTED TO BE SEARCHING FOR THE *DEVICE* THAT THE MAN WHO CALLED HIMSELF "SHERIDAN" WANTED TO FIND.

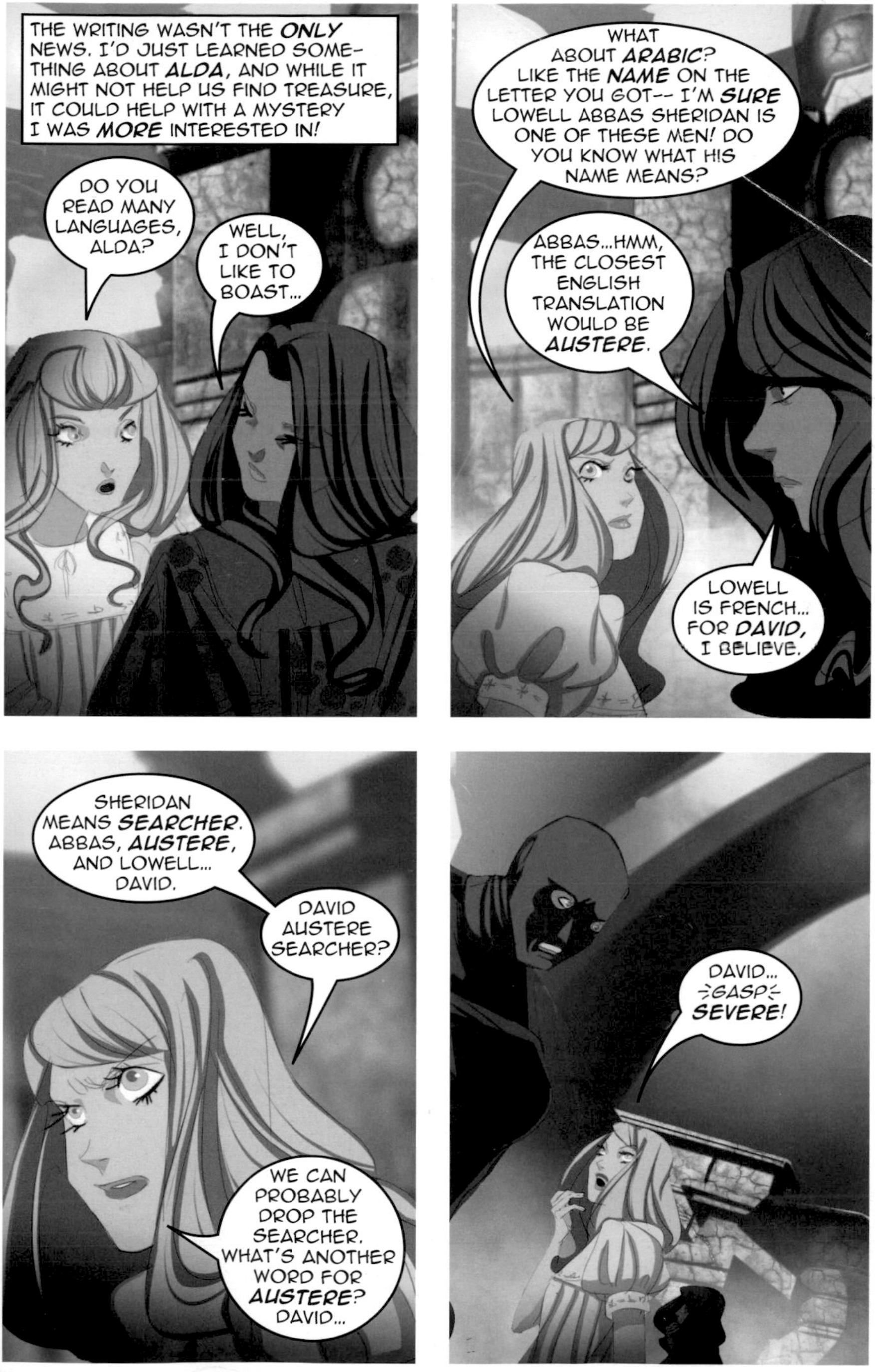
THE WRITING WASN'T THE ONLY NEWS. I'D JUST LEARNED SOMETHING ABOUT ALDA, AND WHILE IT MIGHT NOT HELP US FIND TREASURE, IT COULD HELP WITH A MYSTERY I WAS MORE INTERESTED IN!
DO YOU READ MANY LANGUAGES, ALDA?
WELL, I DON'T LIKE TO BOAST...
WHAT ABOUT ARABIC? LIKE THE NAME ON THE LETTER YOU GOT-- I'M SURE LOWELL ABBAS SHERIDAN IS ONE OF THESE MEN! DO YOU KNOW WHAT HIS NAME MEANS?
ABBAS...HMM, THE CLOSEST ENGLISH TRANSLATION WOULD BE AUSTERE.
LOWELL IS FRENCH... FOR DAVID, I BELIEVE.
SHERIDAN MEANS SEARCHER. ABBAS, AUSTERE, AND LOWELL... DAVID.
DAVID AUSTERE SEARCHER?
WE CAN PROBABLY DROP THE SEARCHER. WHAT'S ANOTHER WORD FOR AUSTERE? DAVID...
DAVID... GASP SEVERE!

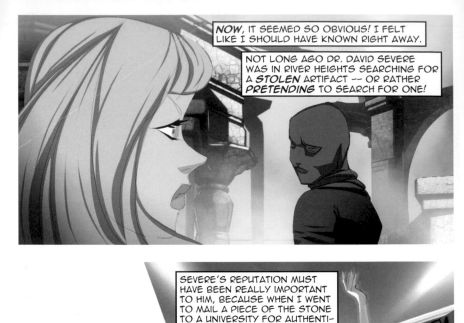

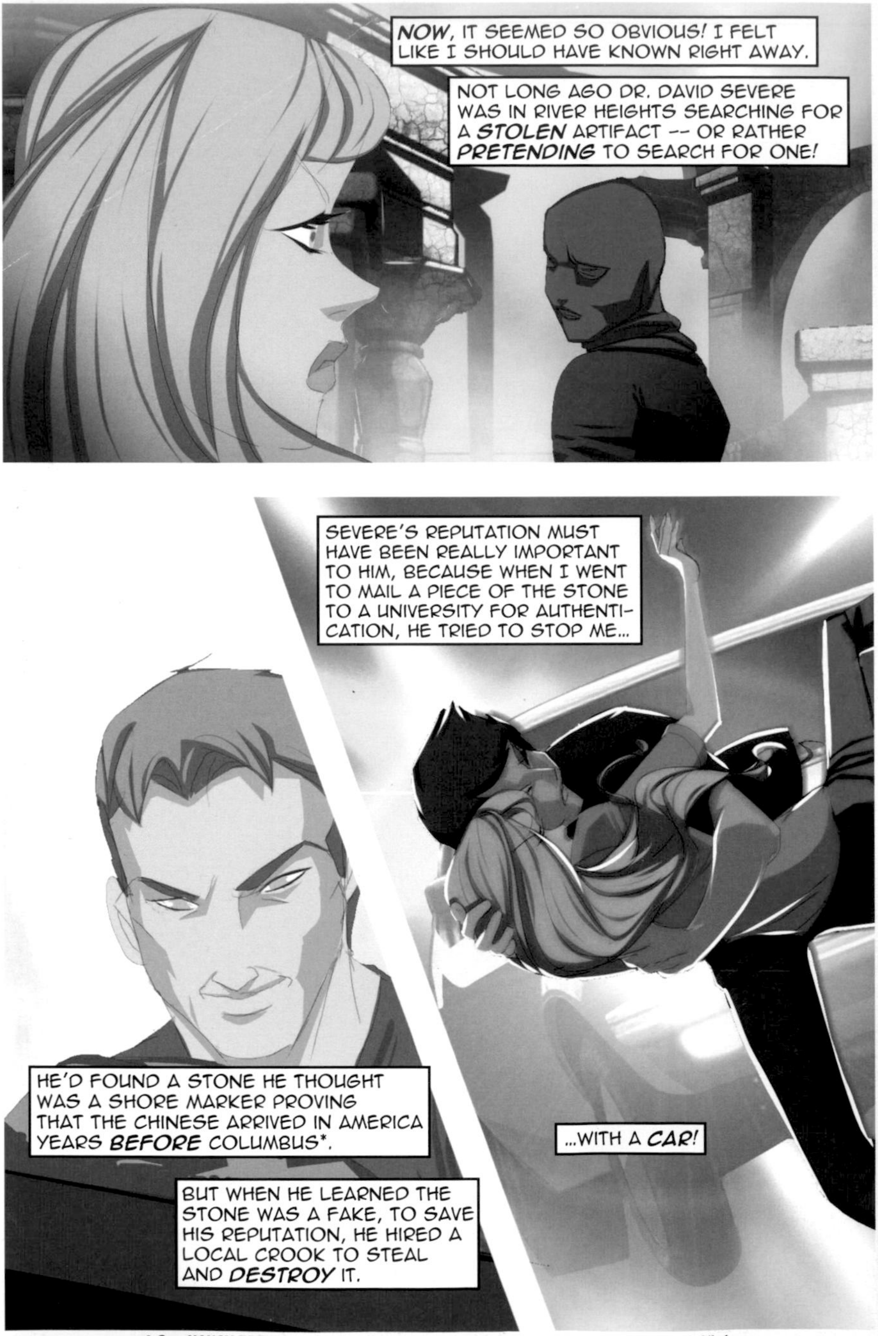
NOW, IT SEEMED SO OBVIOUS! I FELT LIKE I SHOULD HAVE KNOWN RIGHT AWAY.
NOT LONG AGO DR. DAVID SEVERE WAS IN RIVER HEIGHTS SEARCHING FOR A STOLEN ARTIFACT -- OR RATHER PRETENDING TO SEARCH FOR ONE!
HE'D FOUND A STONE HE THOUGHT WAS A SHORE MARKER PROVING THAT THE CHINESE ARRIVED IN AMERICA YEARS BEFORE COLUMBUS*.
BUT WHEN HE LEARNED THE STONE WAS A FAKE, TO SAVE HIS REPUTATION, HE HIRED A LOCAL CROOK TO STEAL AND DESTROY IT.
SEVERE'S REPUTATION MUST HAVE BEEN REALLY IMPORTANT TO HIM, BECAUSE WHEN I WENT TO MAIL A PIECE OF THE STONE TO A UNIVERSITY FOR AUTHENTICATION, HE TRIED TO STOP ME...
...WITH A CAR!

*See NANCY DREW Graphic Novel #2 "Writ in Stone" or go to www.papercutz.com/nd/fn1

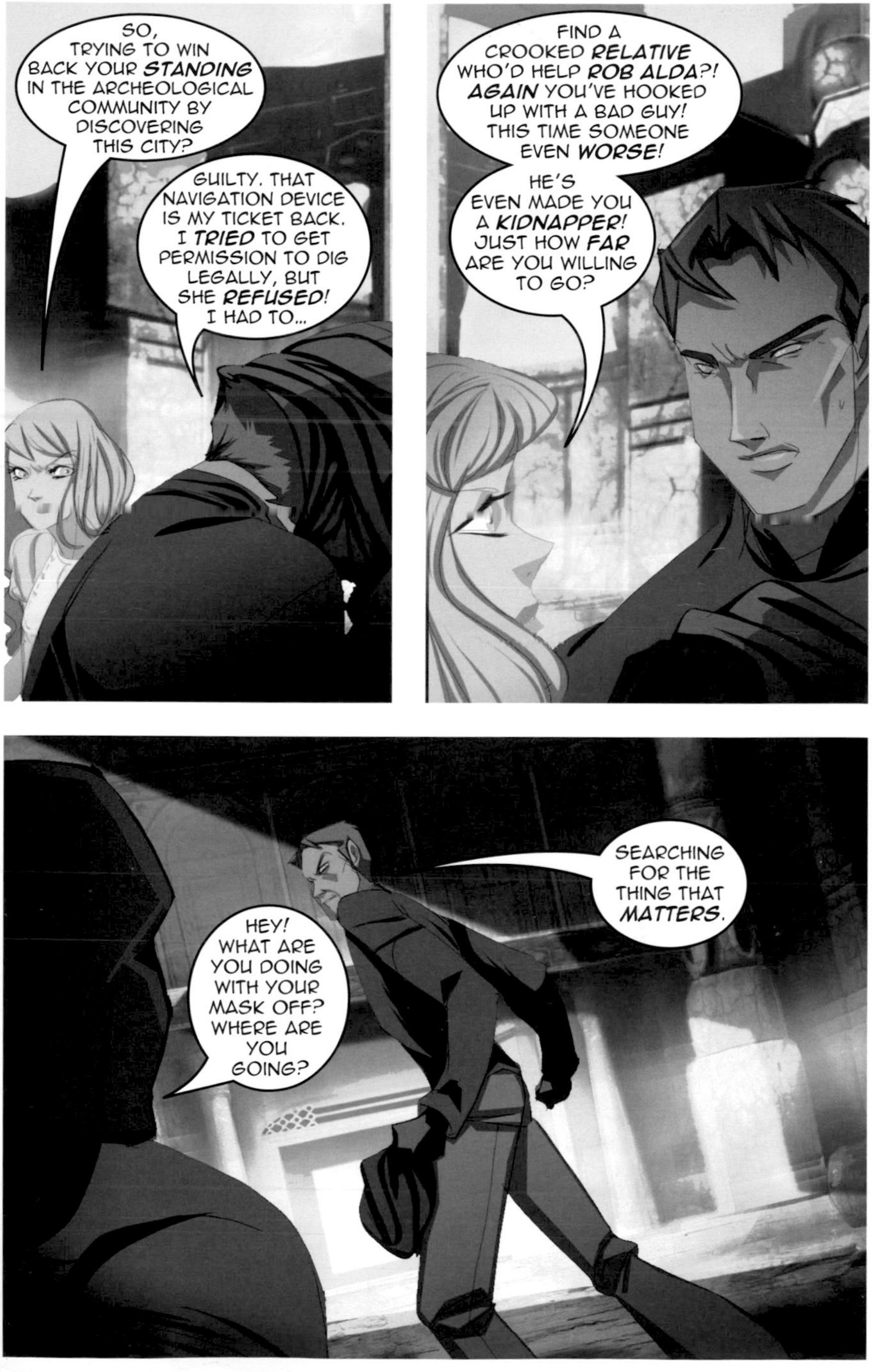
SO, TRYING TO WIN BACK YOUR STANDING IN THE ARCHEOLOGICAL COMMUNITY BY DISCOVERING THIS CITY?
GUILTY. THAT NAVIGATION DEVICE IS MY TICKET BACK. I TRIED TO GET PERMISSION TO DIG LEGALLY, BUT SHE REFUSED! I HAD TO...
FIND A CROOKED RELATIVE WHO'D HELP ROB ALDA?! AGAIN YOU'VE HOOKED UP WITH A BAD GUY! THIS TIME SOMEONE EVEN WORSE!
HE'S EVEN MADE YOU A KIDNAPPER! JUST HOW FAR ARE YOU WILLING TO GO?
HEY! WHAT ARE YOU DOING WITH YOUR MASK OFF? WHERE ARE YOU GOING?
SEARCHING FOR THE THING THAT MATTERS.

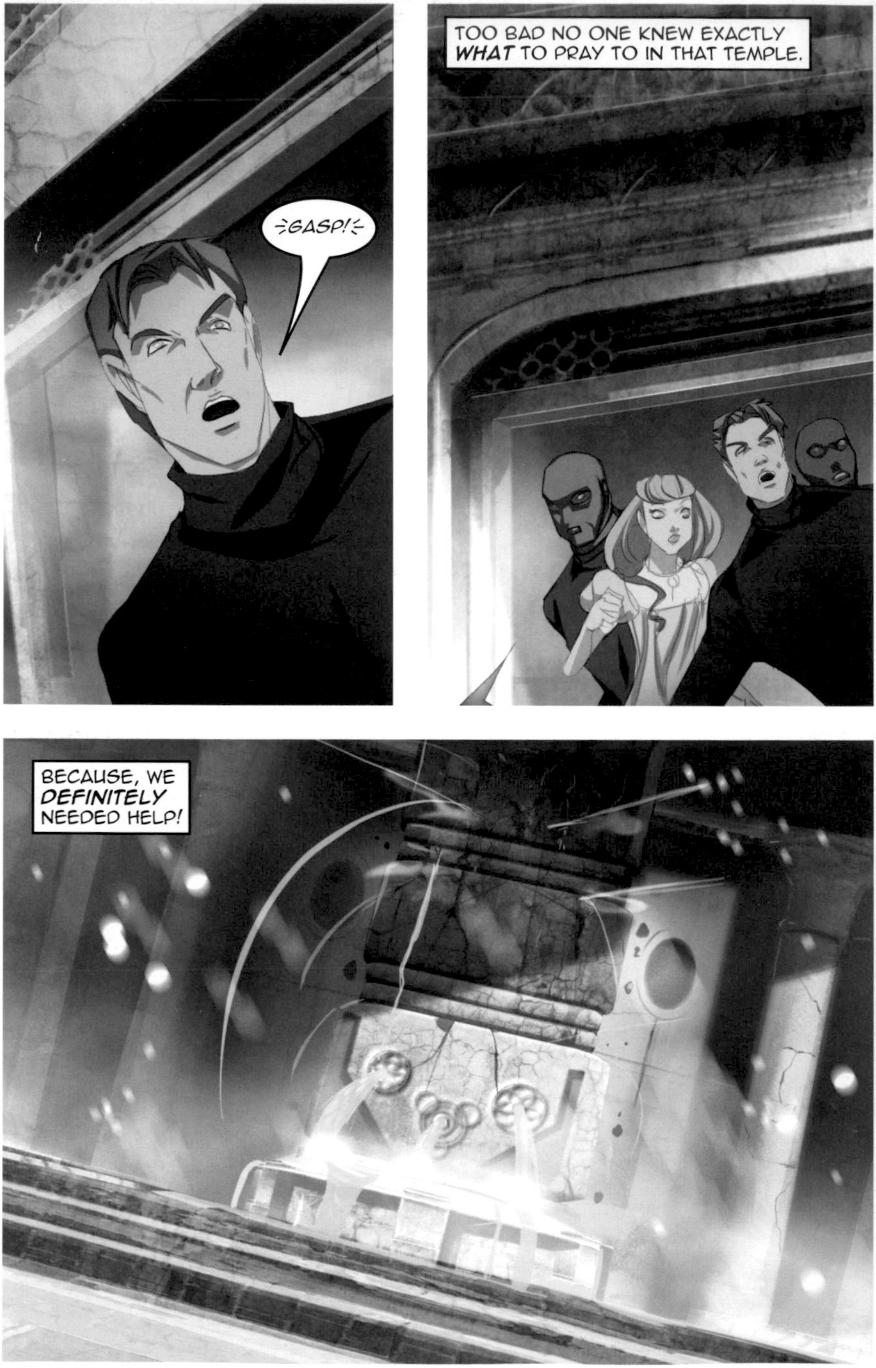
GASP!
TOO BAD NO ONE KNEW EXACTLY *WHAT* TO PRAY TO IN THAT TEMPLE.
BECAUSE, WE *DEFINITELY* NEEDED HELP!

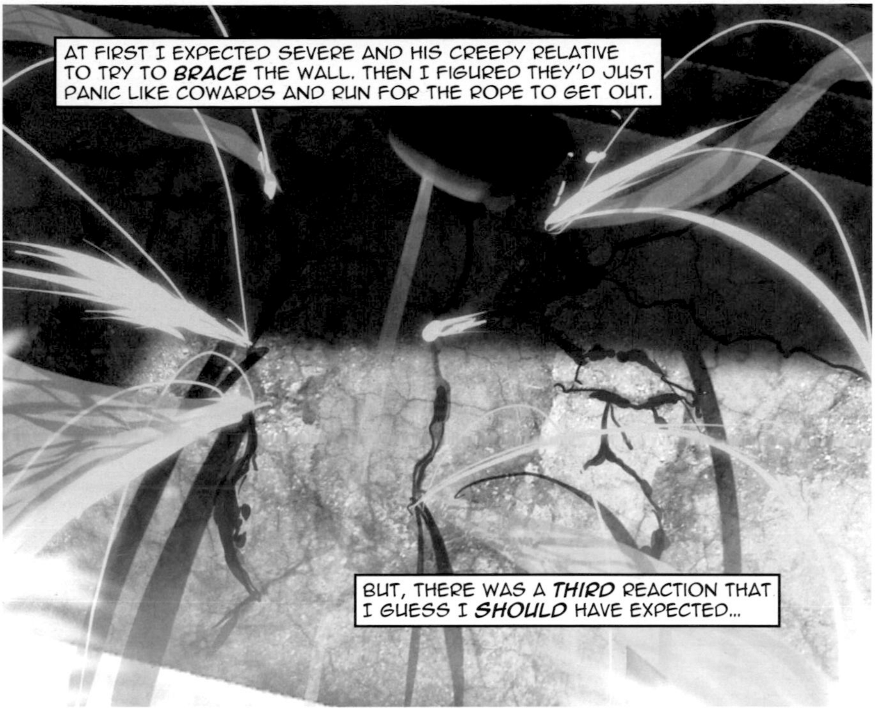
AT FIRST I EXPECTED SEVERE AND HIS CREEPY RELATIVE TO TRY TO *BRACE* THE WALL. THEN I FIGURED THEY'D JUST PANIC LIKE COWARDS AND RUN FOR THE ROPE TO GET OUT.
BUT, THERE WAS A *THIRD* REACTION THAT I GUESS I *SHOULD* HAVE EXPECTED...

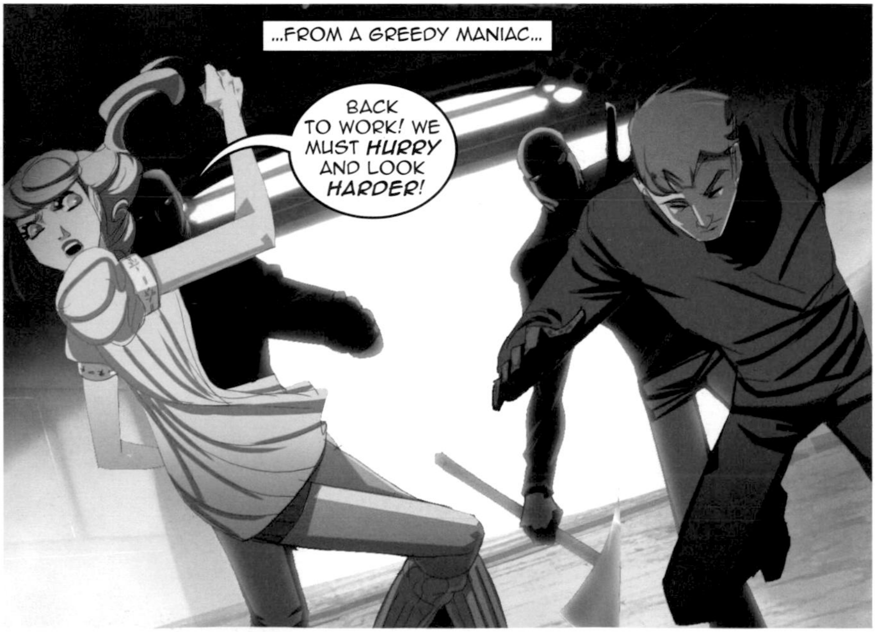
...FROM A GREEDY MANIAC...
BACK TO WORK! WE MUST *HURRY* AND LOOK *HARDER*!

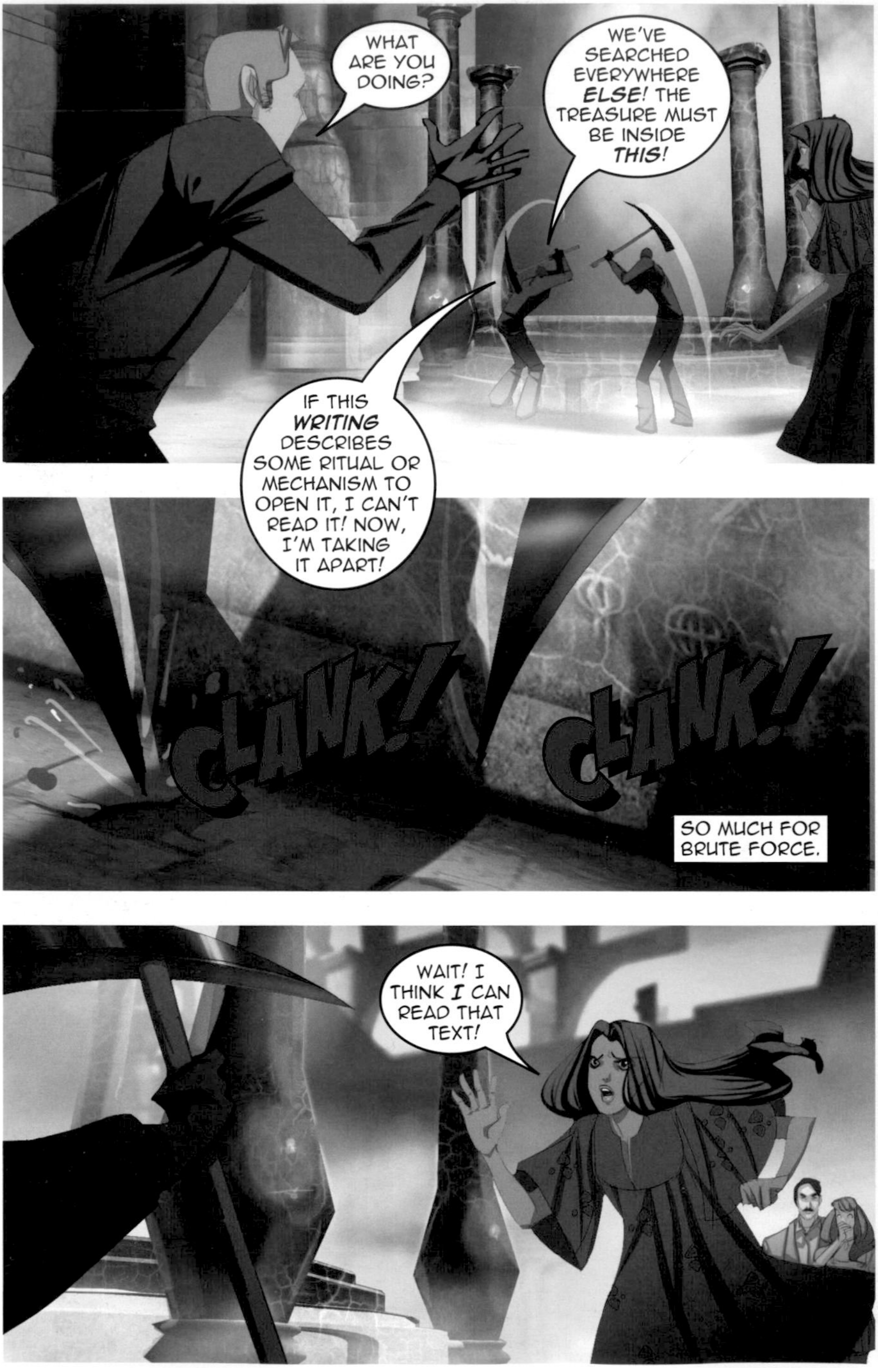

WHAT ARE YOU DOING?
WE'VE SEARCHED EVERYWHERE ELSE! THE TREASURE MUST BE INSIDE THIS!
IF THIS WRITING DESCRIBES SOME RITUAL OR MECHANISM TO OPEN IT, I CAN'T READ IT! NOW, I'M TAKING IT APART!
CLANK!
CLANK!
SO MUCH FOR BRUTE FORCE.
WAIT! I THINK I CAN READ THAT TEXT!

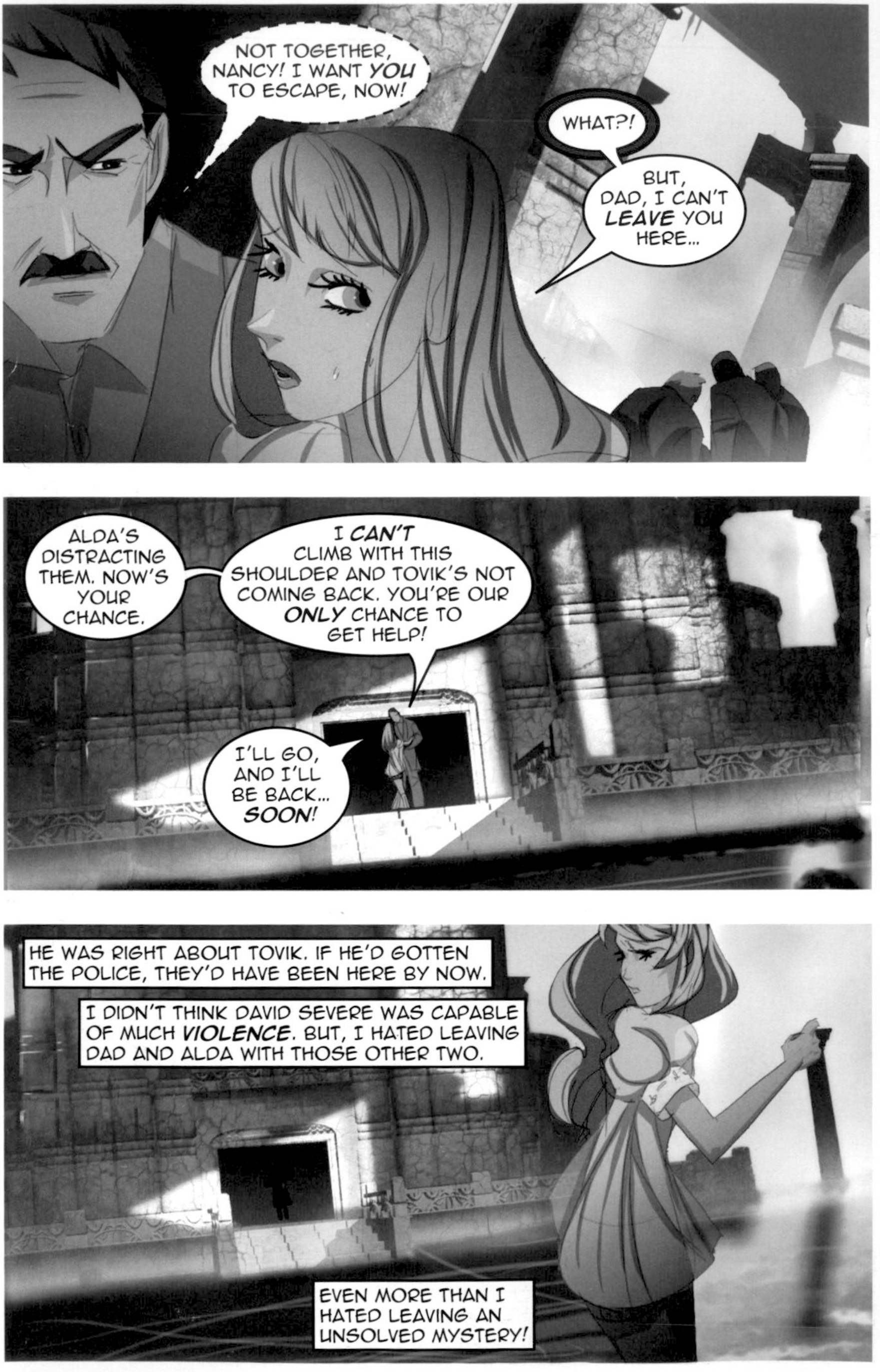
NOT TOGETHER, NANCY! I WANT *YOU* TO ESCAPE, NOW!
WHAT?!
BUT, DAD, I CAN'T *LEAVE* YOU HERE...
ALDA'S DISTRACTING THEM. NOW'S YOUR CHANCE.
I *CAN'T* CLIMB WITH THIS SHOULDER AND TOVIK'S NOT COMING BACK. YOU'RE OUR *ONLY* CHANCE TO GET HELP!
I'LL GO, AND I'LL BE BACK... *SOON*!
HE WAS RIGHT ABOUT TOVIK. IF HE'D GOTTEN THE POLICE, THEY'D HAVE BEEN HERE BY NOW.
I DIDN'T THINK DAVID SEVERE WAS CAPABLE OF MUCH *VIOLENCE*. BUT, I HATED LEAVING DAD AND ALDA WITH THOSE OTHER TWO.
EVEN MORE THAN I HATED LEAVING AN UNSOLVED MYSTERY!

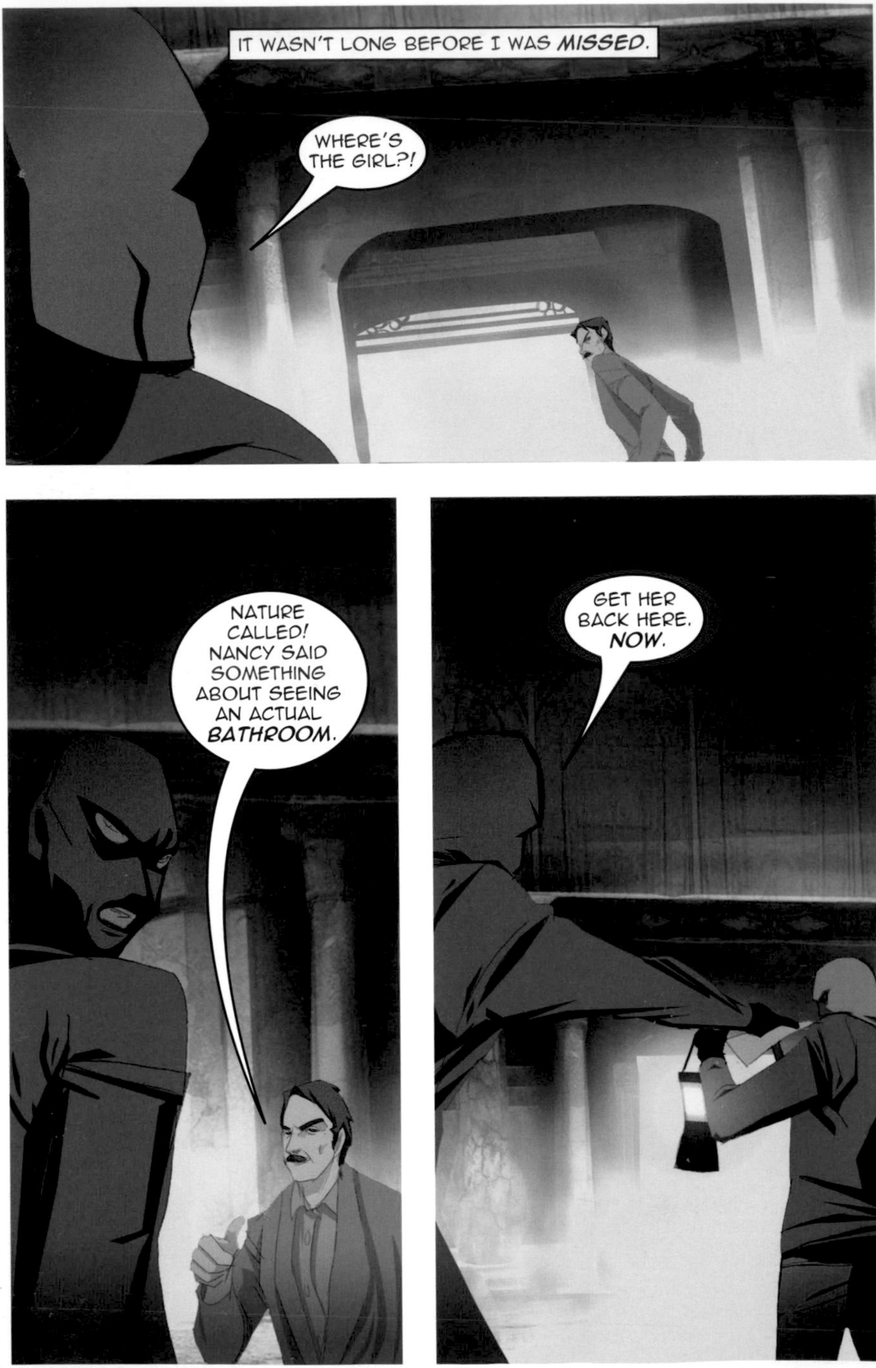
IT WASN'T LONG BEFORE I WAS MISSED.
WHERE'S THE GIRL?!
NATURE CALLED! NANCY SAID SOMETHING ABOUT SEEING AN ACTUAL BATHROOM.
GET HER BACK HERE. NOW.

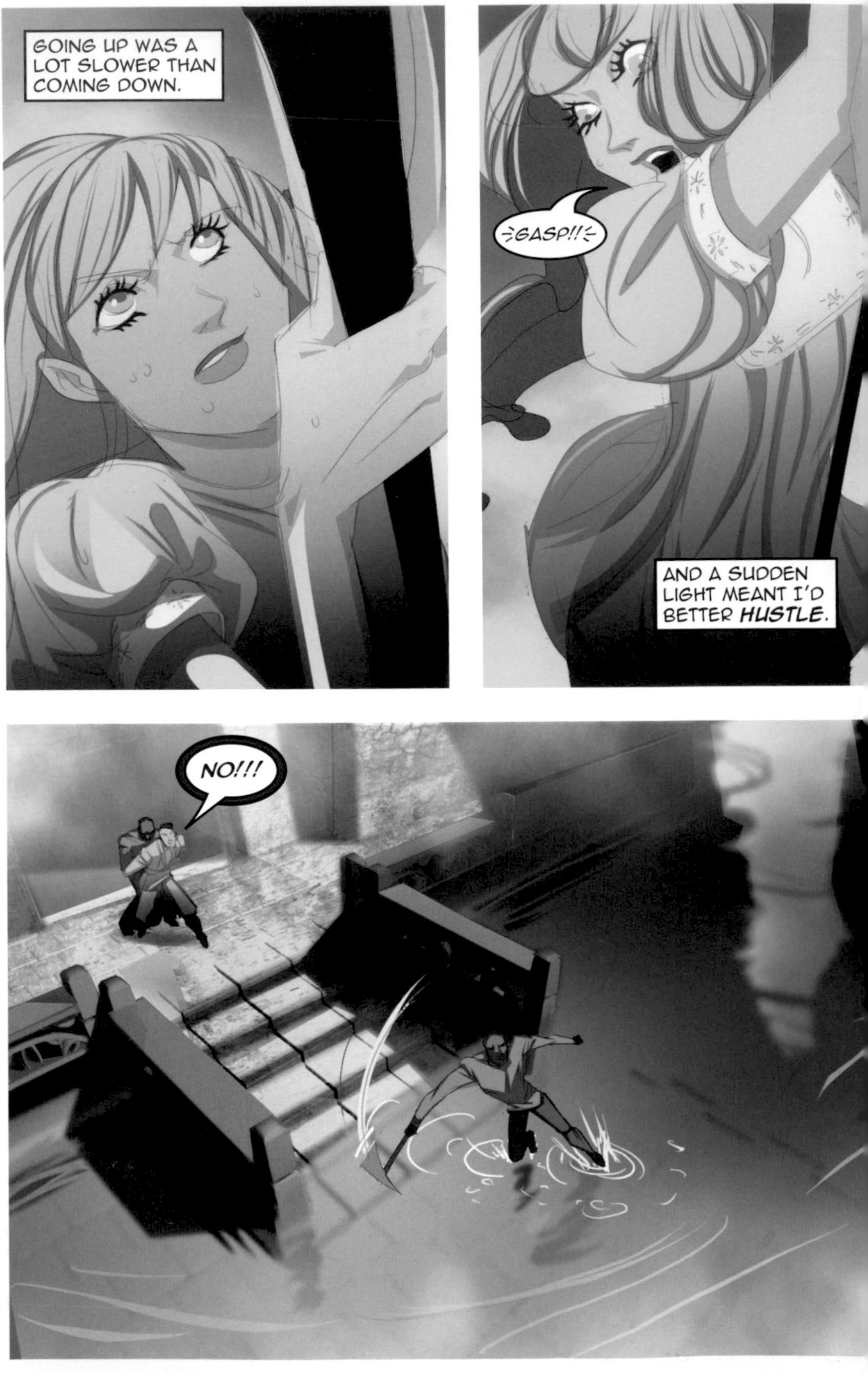
GOING UP WAS A LOT SLOWER THAN COMING DOWN.
GASP!!
AND A SUDDEN LIGHT MEANT I'D BETTER HUSTLE.
NO!!!

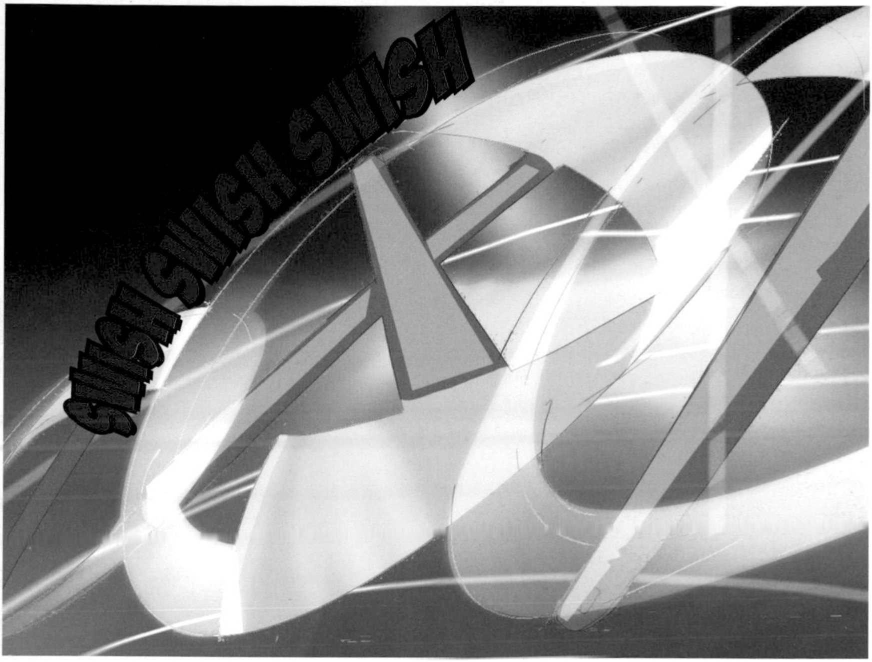
SWISH SWISH SWISH

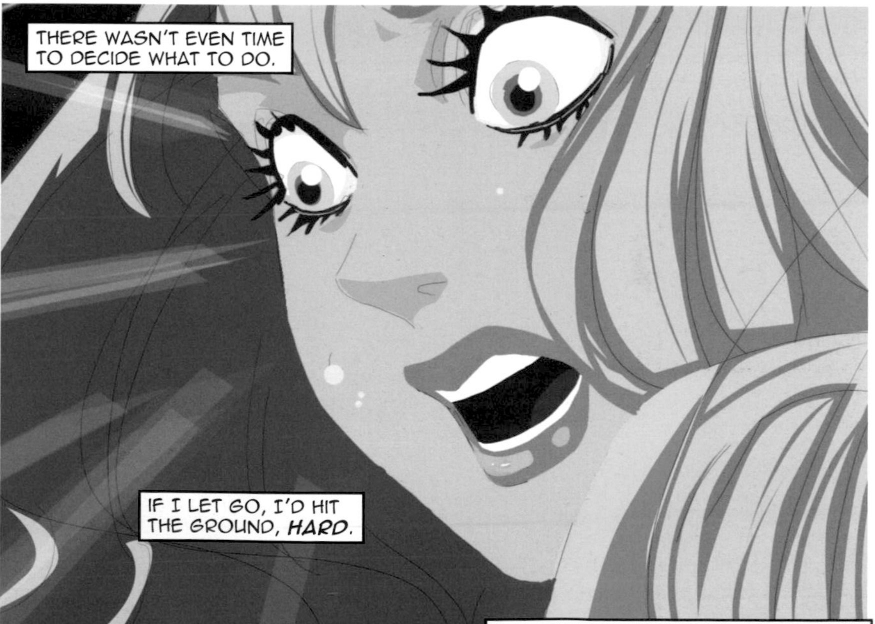
THERE WASN'T EVEN TIME TO DECIDE WHAT TO DO.
IF I LET GO, I'D HIT THE GROUND, *HARD*.
IF I KEPT GOING, THERE WAS NO TELLING WHERE THAT AXE WOULD *HIT*.

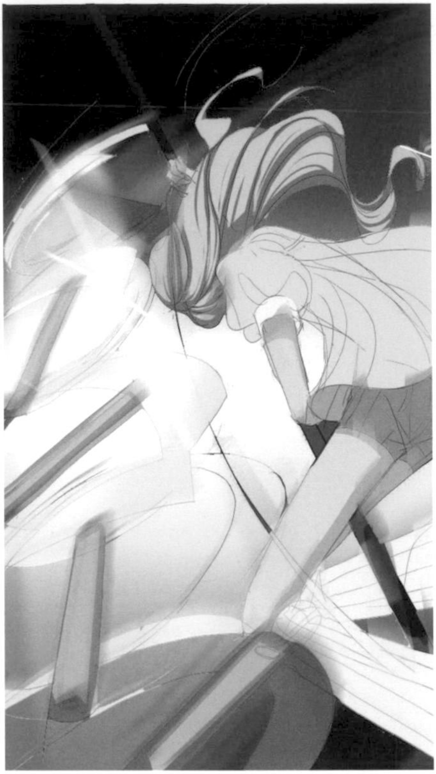

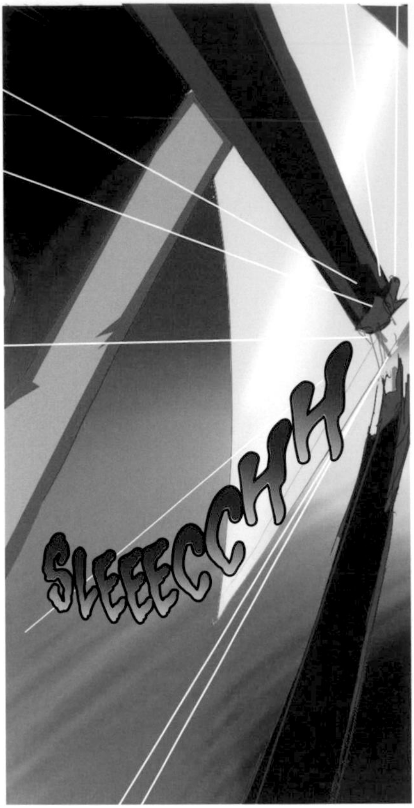
SLEEECCHH

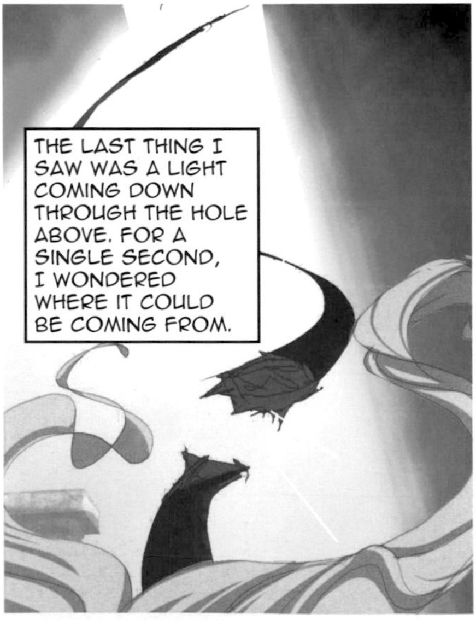
THE LAST THING I SAW WAS A LIGHT COMING DOWN THROUGH THE HOLE ABOVE. FOR A SINGLE SECOND, I WONDERED WHERE IT COULD BE COMING FROM.

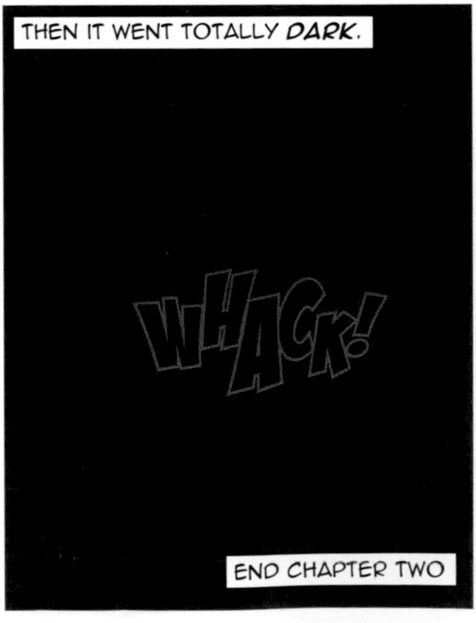
THEN IT WENT TOTALLY DARK.
WHACK!
END CHAPTER TWO

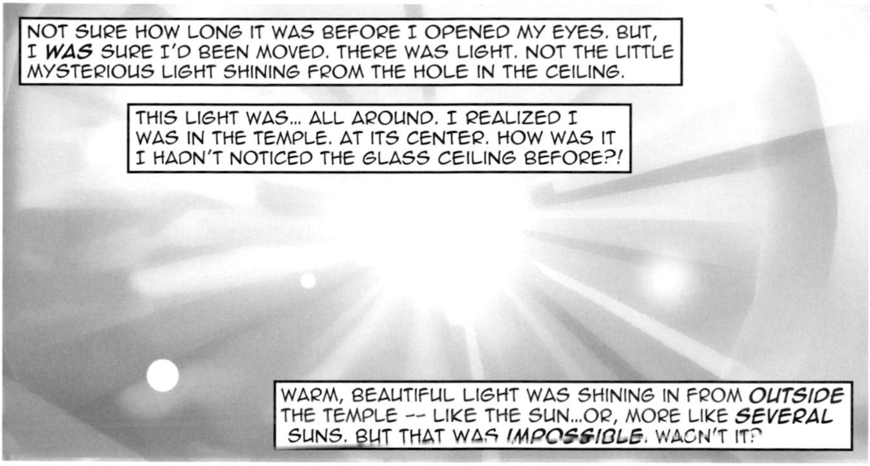
NOT SURE HOW LONG IT WAS BEFORE I OPENED MY EYES. BUT, I WAS SURE I'D BEEN MOVED. THERE WAS LIGHT. NOT THE LITTLE MYSTERIOUS LIGHT SHINING FROM THE HOLE IN THE CEILING.
THIS LIGHT WAS... ALL AROUND. I REALIZED I WAS IN THE TEMPLE. AT ITS CENTER. HOW WAS IT I HADN'T NOTICED THE GLASS CEILING BEFORE?!
WARM, BEAUTIFUL LIGHT WAS SHINING IN FROM OUTSIDE THE TEMPLE -- LIKE THE SUN...OR, MORE LIKE SEVERAL SUNS. BUT THAT WAS IMPOSSIBLE. WASN'T IT?

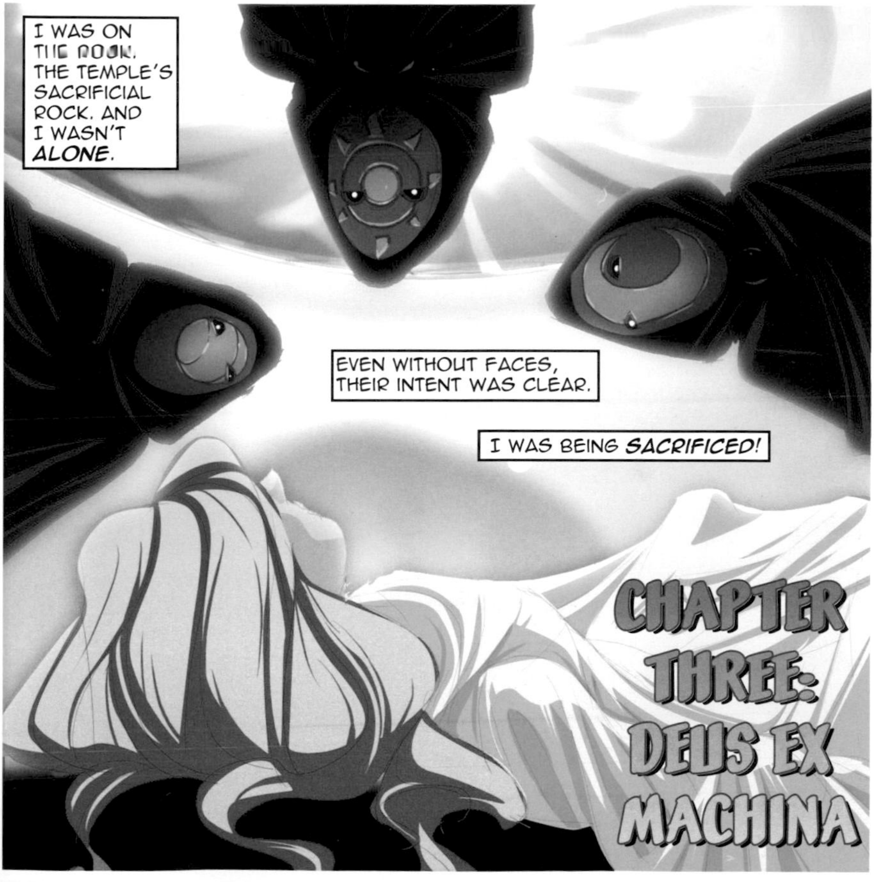
I WAS ON THE ROCK. THE TEMPLE'S SACRIFICIAL ROCK. AND I WASN'T ALONE.
EVEN WITHOUT FACES, THEIR INTENT WAS CLEAR.
I WAS BEING SACRIFICED!
CHAPTER THREE: DEUS EX MACHINA

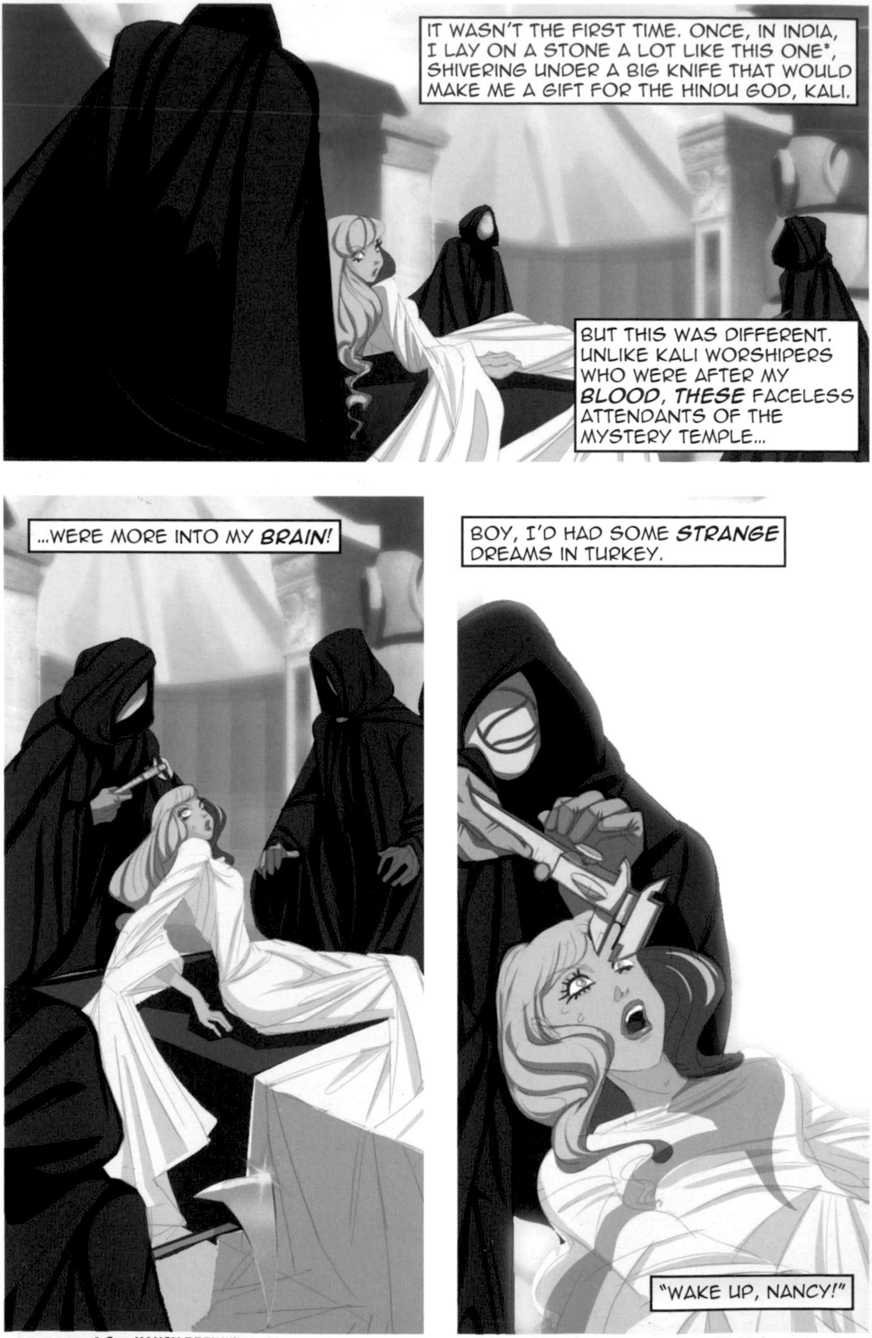
IT WASN'T THE FIRST TIME. ONCE, IN INDIA, I LAY ON A STONE A LOT LIKE THIS ONE*, SHIVERING UNDER A BIG KNIFE THAT WOULD MAKE ME A GIFT FOR THE HINDU GOD, KALI.
BUT THIS WAS DIFFERENT. UNLIKE KALI WORSHIPERS WHO WERE AFTER MY BLOOD, THESE FACELESS ATTENDANTS OF THE MYSTERY TEMPLE...
...WERE MORE INTO MY BRAIN!
BOY, I'D HAD SOME STRANGE DREAMS IN TURKEY.
"WAKE UP, NANCY!"

★ *See NANCY DREW Graphic Novel #4 "The Girl Who Wasn't There" or go to www.papercutz.com/nd/fn2*

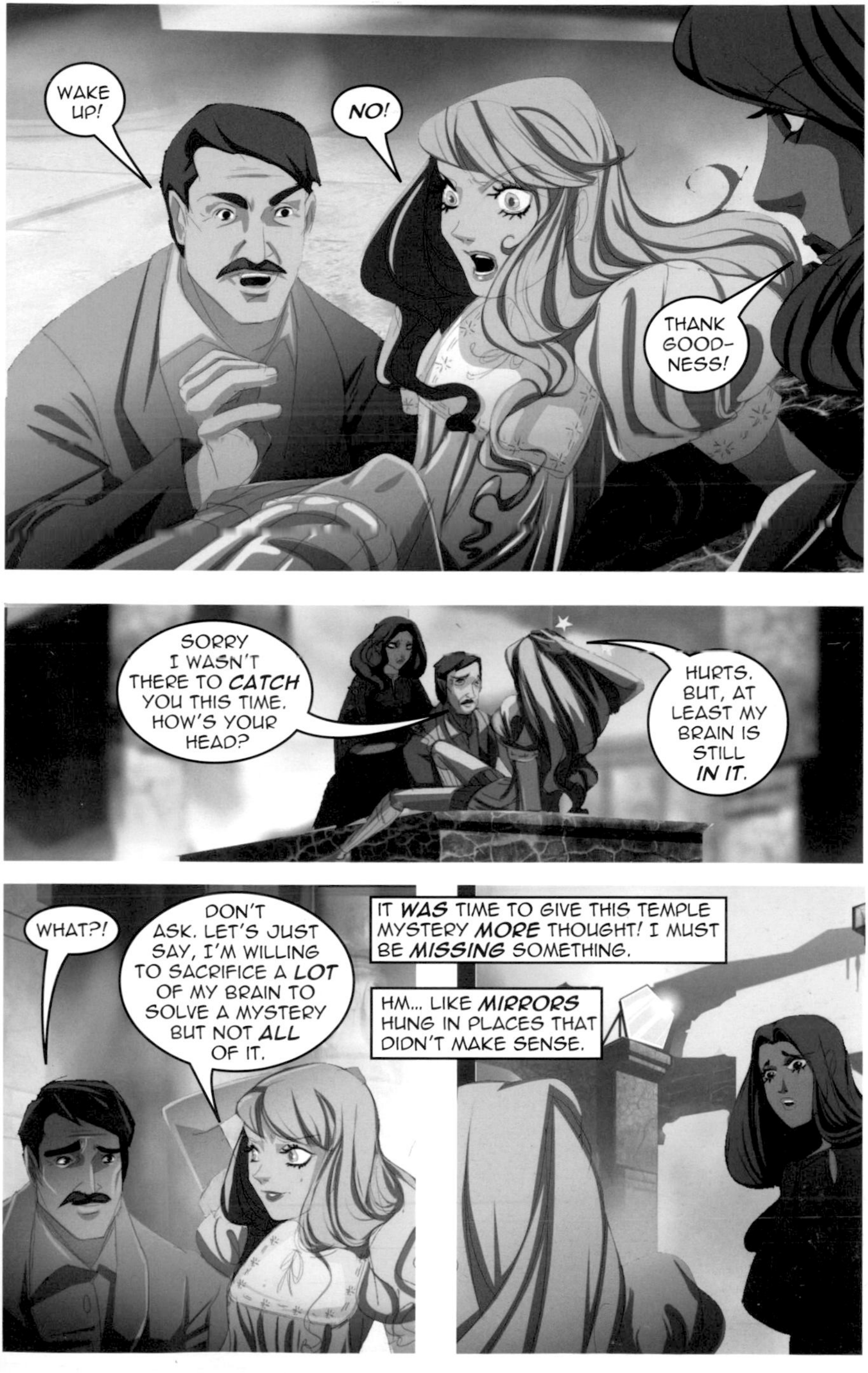
WAKE UP!
NO!
THANK GOOD-NESS!
SORRY I WASN'T THERE TO CATCH YOU THIS TIME. HOW'S YOUR HEAD?
HURTS. BUT, AT LEAST MY BRAIN IS STILL IN IT.
WHAT?!
DON'T ASK. LET'S JUST SAY, I'M WILLING TO SACRIFICE A LOT OF MY BRAIN TO SOLVE A MYSTERY BUT NOT ALL OF IT.
IT WAS TIME TO GIVE THIS TEMPLE MYSTERY MORE THOUGHT! I MUST BE MISSING SOMETHING.
HM... LIKE MIRRORS HUNG IN PLACES THAT DIDN'T MAKE SENSE.

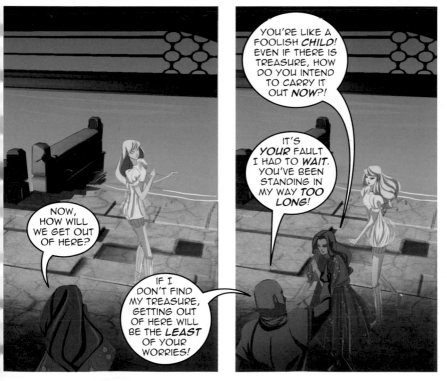

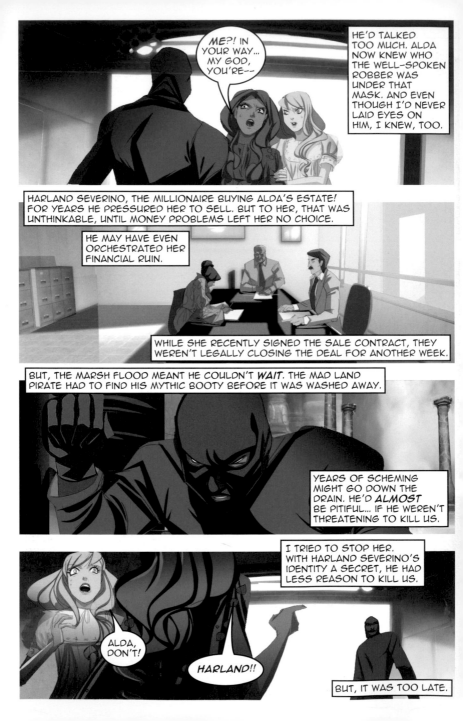

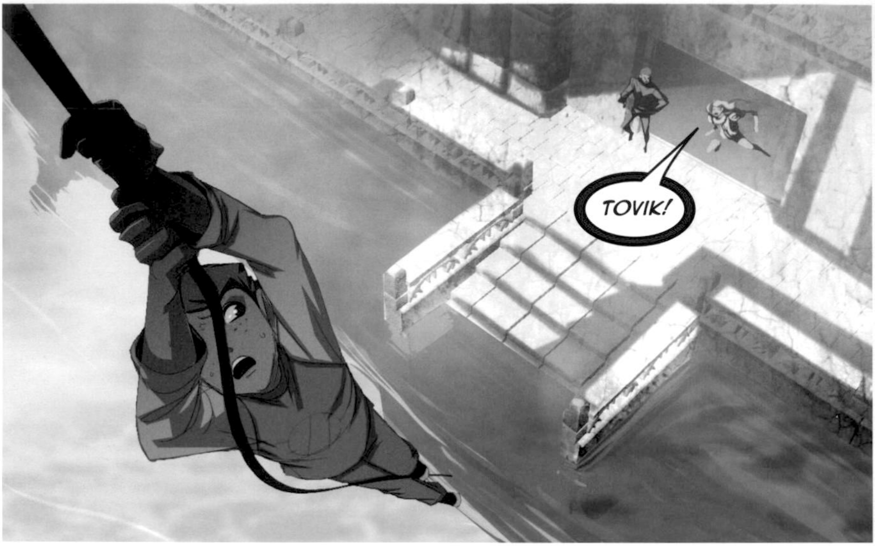
TOVIK!

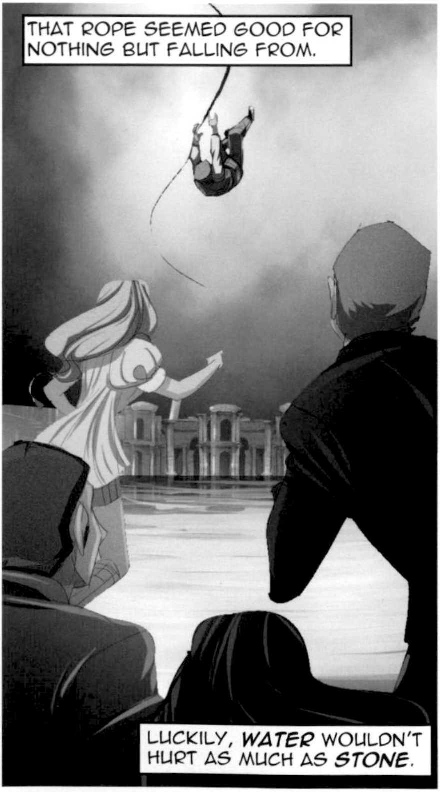
THAT ROPE SEEMED GOOD FOR NOTHING BUT FALLING FROM.
LUCKILY, WATER WOULDN'T HURT AS MUCH AS STONE.

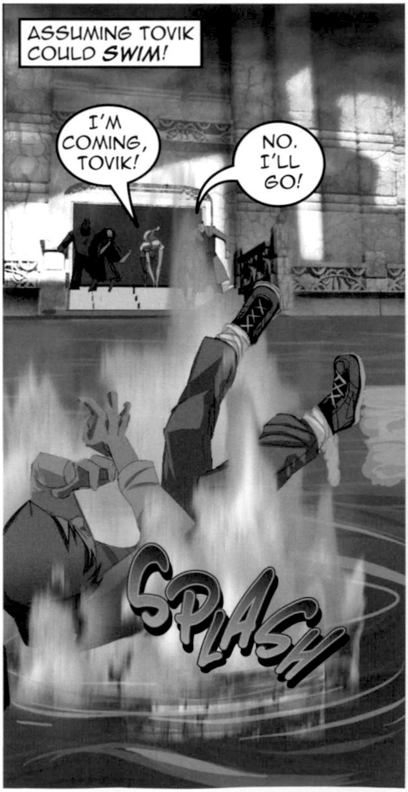
ASSUMING TOVIK COULD SWIM!
I'M COMING, TOVIK!
NO. I'LL GO!
SPLASH

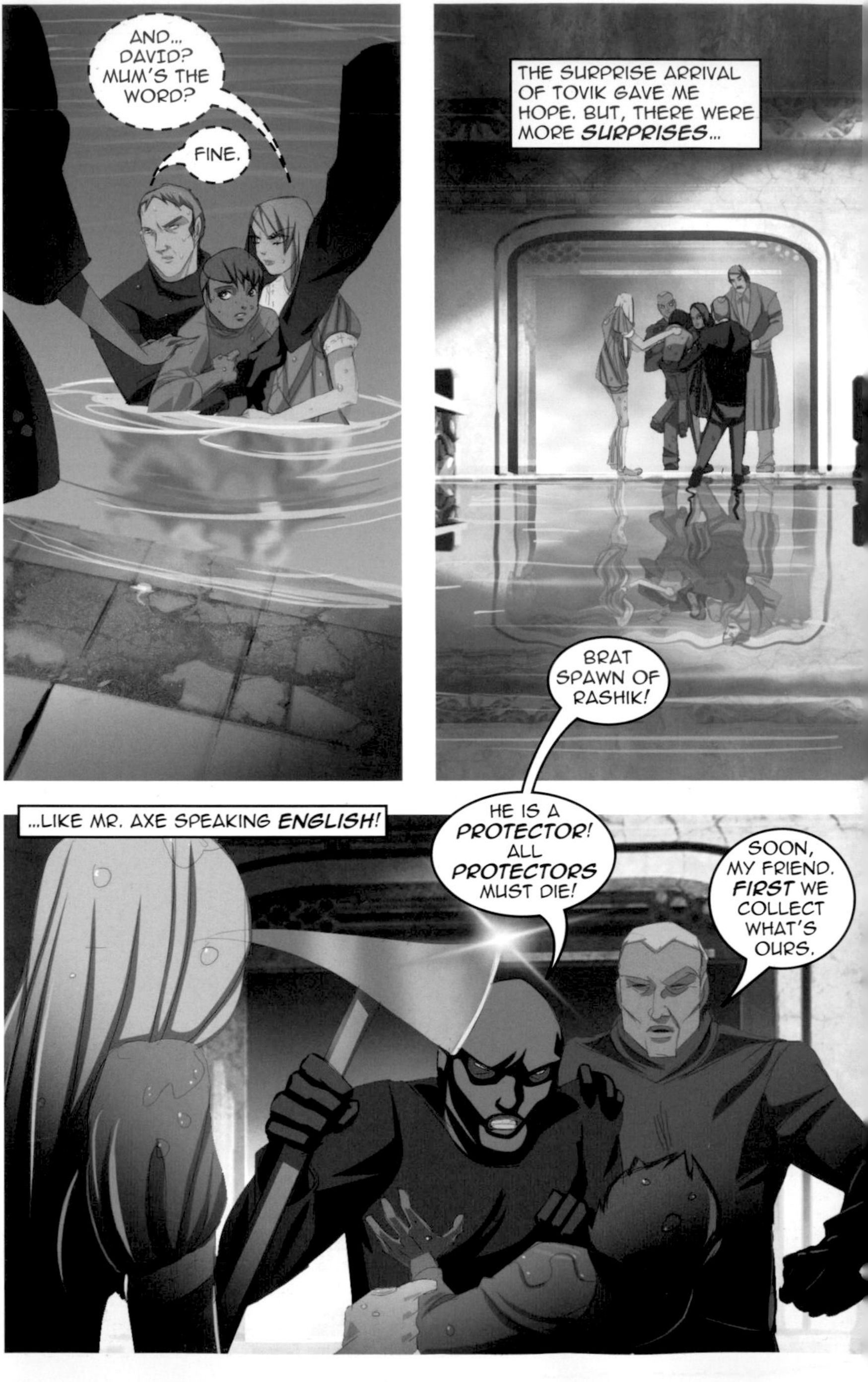
AND... DAVID? MUM'S THE WORD?
FINE.
THE SURPRISE ARRIVAL OF TOVIK GAVE ME HOPE. BUT, THERE WERE MORE SURPRISES...
BRAT SPAWN OF RASHIK!
...LIKE MR. AXE SPEAKING ENGLISH!
HE IS A PROTECTOR! ALL PROTECTORS MUST DIE!
SOON, MY FRIEND. FIRST WE COLLECT WHAT'S OURS.

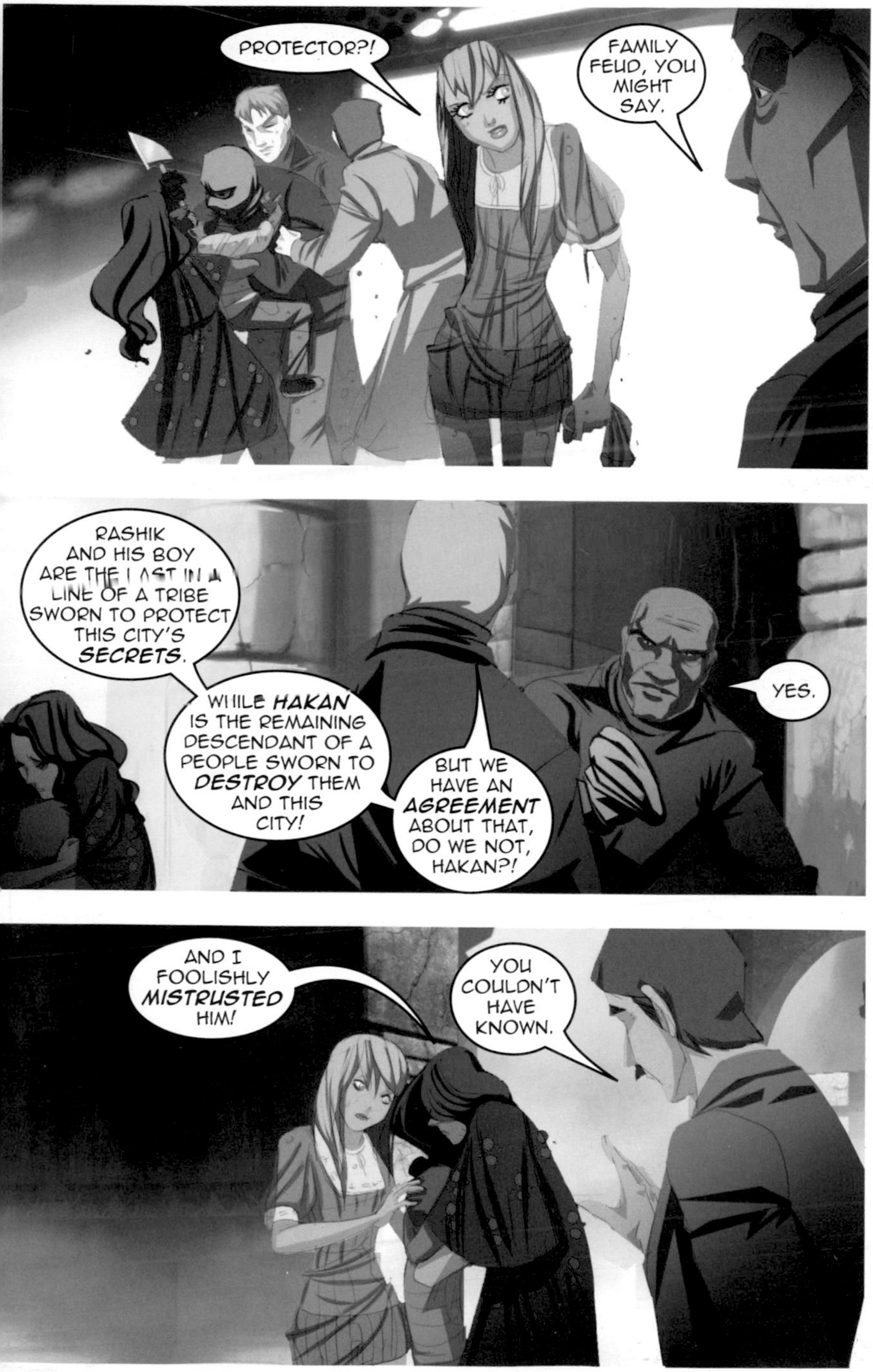
PROTECTOR?!
FAMILY FEUD, YOU MIGHT SAY.
RASHIK AND HIS BOY ARE THE LAST IN A LINE OF A TRIBE SWORN TO PROTECT THIS CITY'S SECRETS.
WHILE HAKAN IS THE REMAINING DESCENDANT OF A PEOPLE SWORN TO DESTROY THEM AND THIS CITY!
BUT WE HAVE AN AGREEMENT ABOUT THAT, DO WE NOT, HAKAN?!
YES.
AND I FOOLISHLY MISTRUSTED HIM!
YOU COULDN'T HAVE KNOWN.

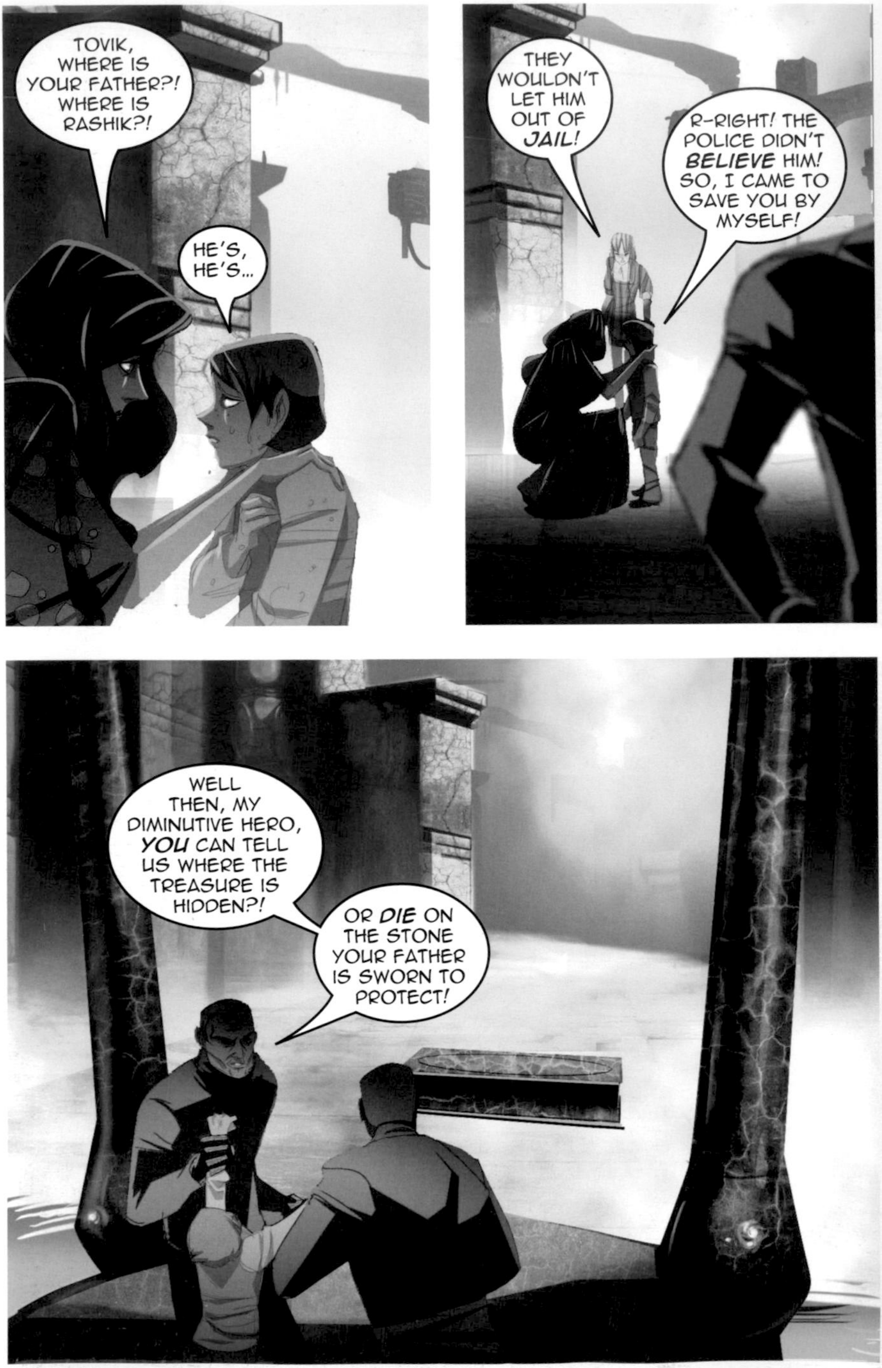

TOVIK, WHERE IS YOUR FATHER?! WHERE IS RASHIK?!
HE'S, HE'S...
THEY WOULDN'T LET HIM OUT OF **JAIL**!
R-RIGHT! THE POLICE DIDN'T **BELIEVE** HIM! SO, I CAME TO SAVE YOU BY MYSELF!
WELL THEN, MY DIMINUTIVE HERO, **YOU** CAN TELL US WHERE THE TREASURE IS HIDDEN?!
OR **DIE** ON THE STONE YOUR FATHER IS SWORN TO PROTECT!

TOVIK TRIGGERED A MECHANISM WHEN HE BOUNCED ON THE STONE. NOW THE SHAKING WATER WASHED AWAY THE MURKY MYSTERY OF THIS PLACE.

LOOK!

MY DREAM *WAS* TELLING ME SOMETHING! THE SECRET WAS IN MY *BRAIN*. IT WAS JUST *COVERED* WITH DUST.

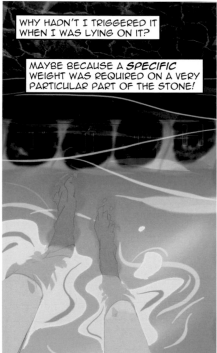

WHY HADN'T I TRIGGERED IT WHEN I WAS LYING ON IT?

MAYBE BECAUSE A *SPECIFIC* WEIGHT WAS REQUIRED ON A VERY PARTICULAR PART OF THE STONE!

A BIT OF A HUNCH. BUT, I'D SOLVED CASES ON *WEAKER* HUNCHES THAN THIS.

QUICKLY, TOVIK! HELP ME CLEAN THE STONE!

NO PROBLEM!

AFTER ALDA TRANSLATED THE NUMERAL STONES, WE FOUND THE PROPER NUMBER TO MATCH THE DATE.

I DIDN'T KNOW *WHAT*, IF ANYTHING, WOULD HAPPEN, BUT WE ALL HELD OUR BREATH AS TOVIK ADDED THE LAST STONE.

CA-CHIK!

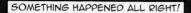

SOMETHING HAPPENED ALL RIGHT!

BENEATH US, WE FELT GEARS TURN, CAUSING THE WHOLE TEMPLE TO SHIFT AND STRAIN, OPENING, MOVING ITS MIRRORS TO MATCH THE POSITION OF THE STARS ON THE DATE WE'D SELECTED!

RUMBLE

WHERE'S THE TREASURE?

THIS IS *IT!* THE TEMPLE! *THIS* IS THE CALCULATOR!

YUP. THE DEVICE DAVID HAD BEEN SEARCHING FOR *WAS* THE TEMPLE ITSELF. AND THE TREASURE...

WELL, THAT WAS THE BRILLIANT AND COLLECTIVE GENIUS THAT CREATED IT.

AND, JUST IN TIME, THE *SUNLIGHT* ARRIVED! ONLY *TROUBLE* WAS, THE BUILDING HADN'T MOVED IN A *REALLY LONG TIME*.

NOW IT WAS RIPPING ITSELF APART!

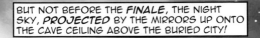
BUT NOT BEFORE THE *FINALE*, THE NIGHT SKY, *PROJECTED* BY THE MIRRORS UP ONTO THE CAVE CEILING ABOVE THE BURIED CITY!

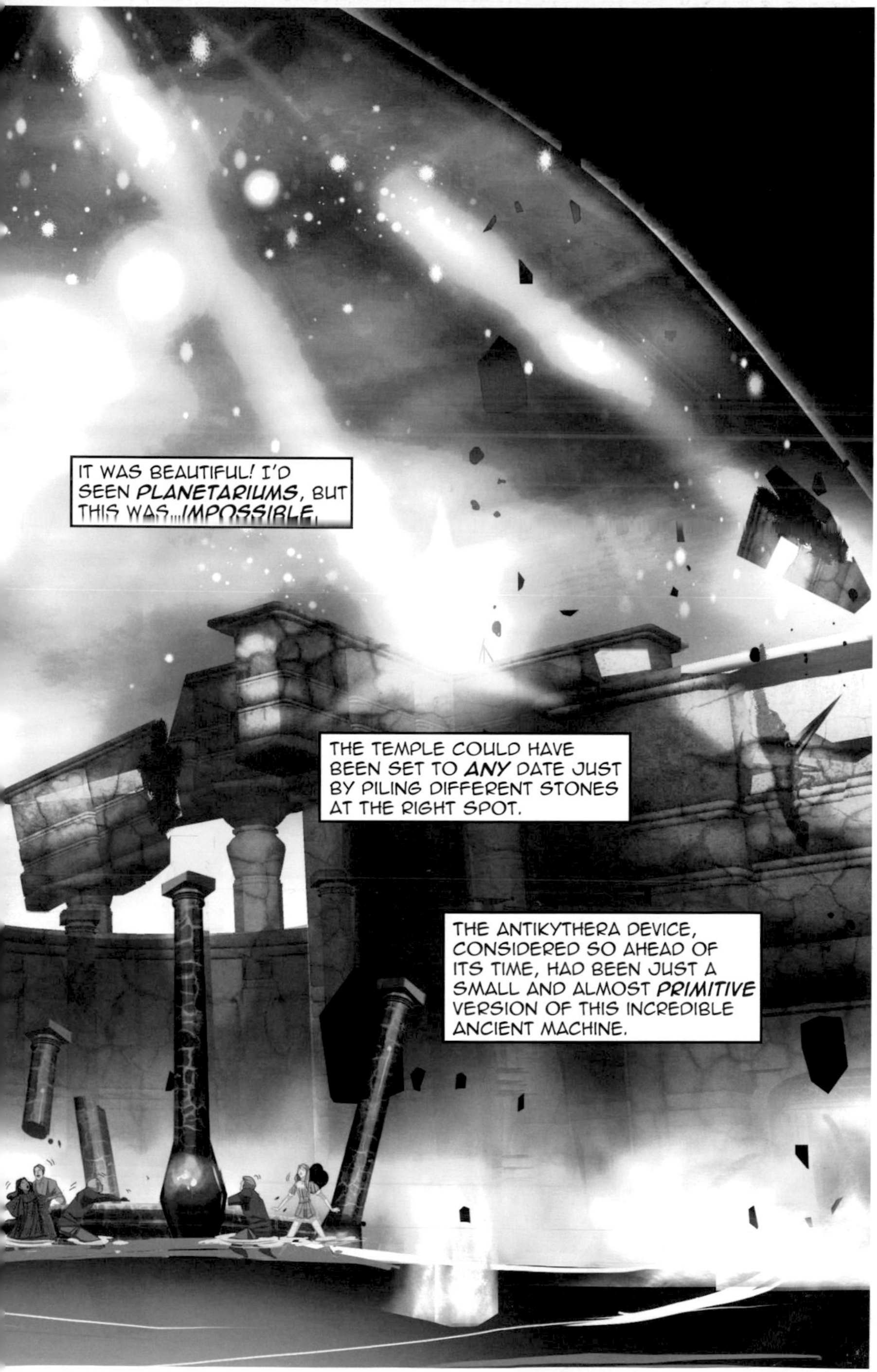
IT WAS BEAUTIFUL! I'D SEEN PLANETARIUMS, BUT THIS WAS...IMPOSSIBLE.
THE TEMPLE COULD HAVE BEEN SET TO ANY DATE JUST BY PILING DIFFERENT STONES AT THE RIGHT SPOT.
THE ANTIKYTHERA DEVICE, CONSIDERED SO AHEAD OF ITS TIME, HAD BEEN JUST A SMALL AND ALMOST PRIMITIVE VERSION OF THIS INCREDIBLE ANCIENT MACHINE.

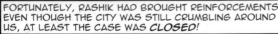

FORTUNATELY, RASHIK HAD BROUGHT REINFORCEMENTS. EVEN THOUGH THE CITY WAS STILL CRUMBLING AROUND US, AT LEAST THE CASE WAS *CLOSED*!

COME ON, DAD! THE BAD GUYS ARE CAUGHT AND THE POLICE HAVE A WINCH ABOVE THE SHAFT TO PULL US OUT!

YES, YES. TIME TO GO.

SO, POOR DAD HAD GOTTEN A TOUGH LESSON ABOUT LOVE. I GUESS IT NEVER GETS EASY.

BUT THE LESSON DAVID SEVERE LEARNED SEEMED LIKE A GOOD ONE!

JUST SEEING THAT AMAZING DEVICE WAS A GREATER TREASURE THAN I COULD HAVE HOPED FOR! I'M ONLY SORRY I *EVER* LISTENED TO YOU!

YOU'RE AN IDIOT!

BUT SOME PEOPLE *NEVER* CHANGE.

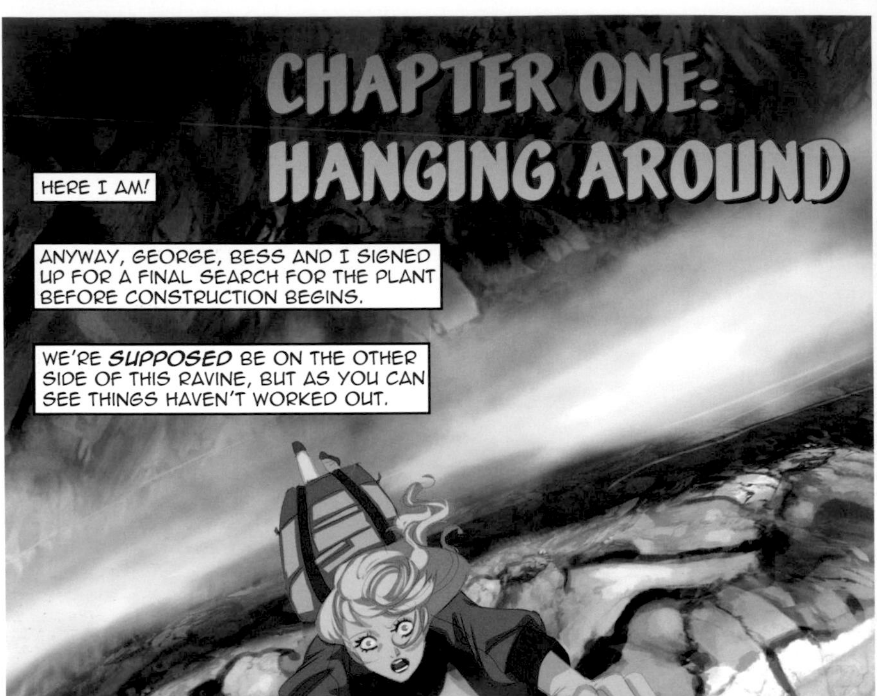
CHAPTER ONE:
HANGING AROUND
HERE I AM!
ANYWAY, GEORGE, BESS AND I SIGNED UP FOR A FINAL SEARCH FOR THE PLANT BEFORE CONSTRUCTION BEGINS.
WE'RE SUPPOSED BE ON THE OTHER SIDE OF THIS RAVINE, BUT AS YOU CAN SEE THINGS HAVEN'T WORKED OUT.
LAST TIME I WAS IN A SITUATION LIKE THIS, IT WAS FOR A MOVIE*.

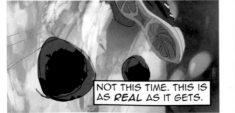

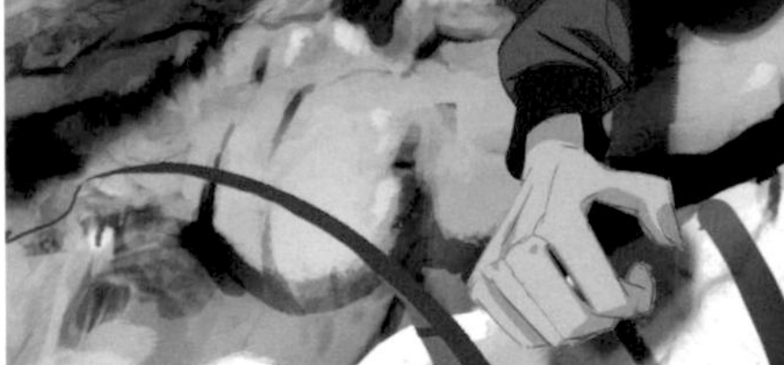
NOT THIS TIME. THIS IS AS REAL AS IT GETS.

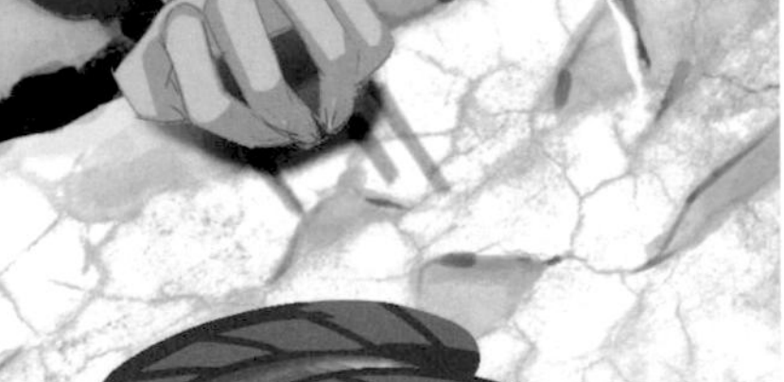
POT!
AND IT'S REALLY MY OWN DARN FAULT!

*See NANCY DREW Graphic Novel #1 "The Demon of River Heights" or go to www.papercutz.com/nd/fn3

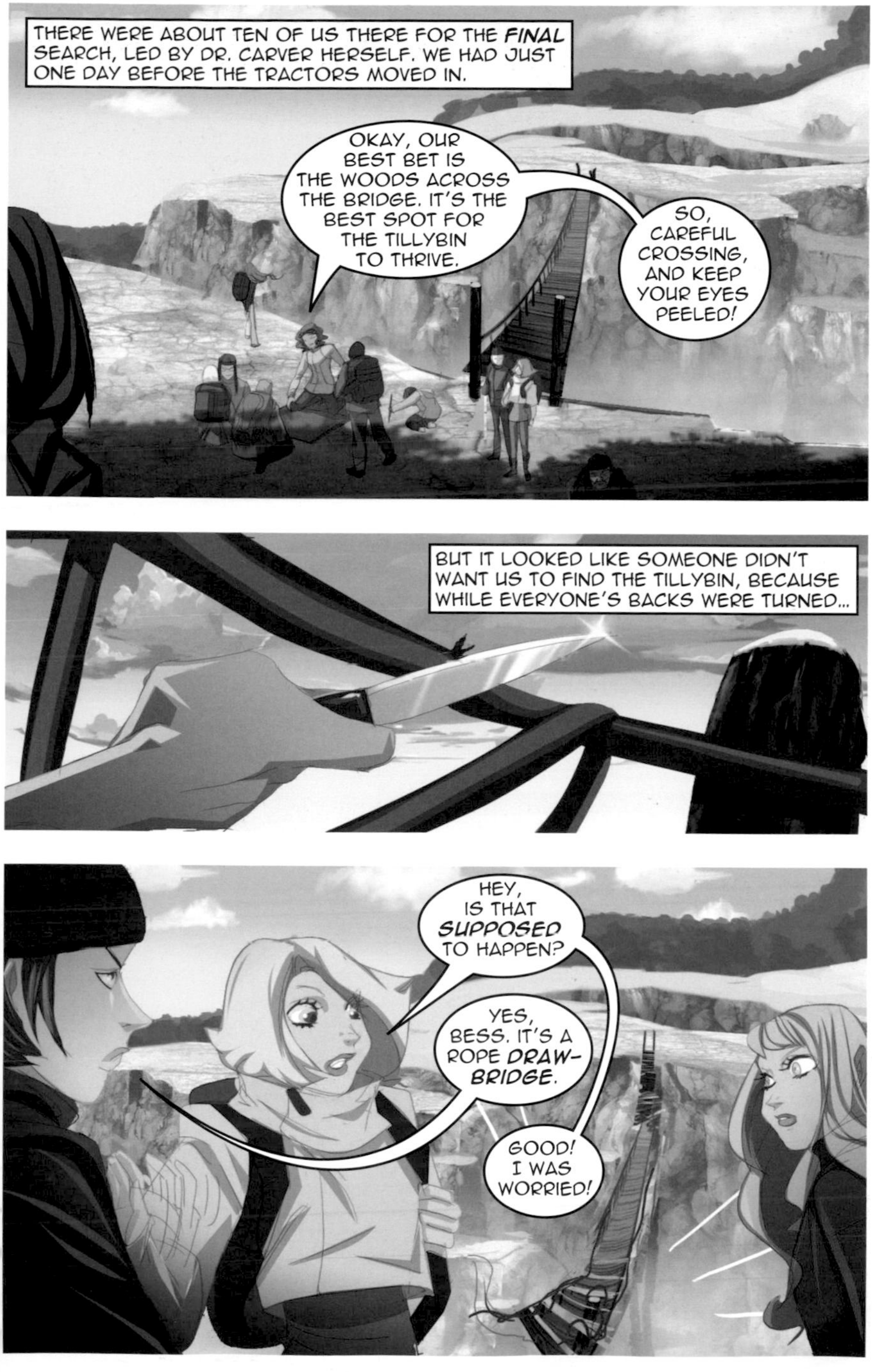

THERE WERE ABOUT TEN OF US THERE FOR THE *FINAL* SEARCH, LED BY DR. CARVER HERSELF. WE HAD JUST ONE DAY BEFORE THE TRACTORS MOVED IN.
OKAY, OUR BEST BET IS THE WOODS ACROSS THE BRIDGE. IT'S THE BEST SPOT FOR THE TILLYBIN TO THRIVE.
SO, CAREFUL CROSSING, AND KEEP YOUR EYES PEELED!
BUT IT LOOKED LIKE SOMEONE DIDN'T WANT US TO FIND THE TILLYBIN, BECAUSE WHILE EVERYONE'S BACKS WERE TURNED...
HEY, IS THAT *SUPPOSED* TO HAPPEN?
YES, BESS. IT'S A ROPE ***DRAW-BRIDGE***.
GOOD! I WAS WORRIED!

DON'T MISS NANCY DREW GRAPHIC NOVEL #19 – "CLIFFHANGER"

THE HARDY BOYS

A NEW GRAPHIC NOVEL EVERY 3 MONTHS!

#13 "The Deadliest Stunt"
ISBN - 978-1-59707-102-4
#14 "Haley Danielle's Top Eight!"
ISBN - 978-1-59707-113-0
#15 "Live Free, Die Hardy!"
ISBN - 978-1-59707-123-9
#16 "SHHHHHH!"
ISBN - 978-1-59707-138-3
NEW! #17 "Word Up!"
ISBN - 978-1-59707-147-5
Also available - Hardy Boys #1-12
All: Pocket sized, 96-112 pp., full-color, $7.95
Also available in hardcover! $12.95

NEW!

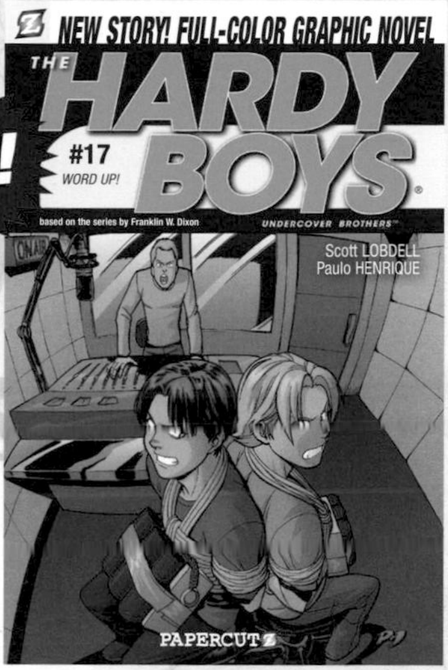
NEW STORY! FULL-COLOR GRAPHIC NOVEL
THE HARDY BOYS
#17
WORD UP!
based on the series by Franklin W. Dixon
UNDERCOVER BROTHERS
Scott LOBDELL
Paulo HENRIQUE
PAPERCUTZ

THE HARDY BOYS BOXED SETS
#1-4 ISBN - 978-1-59707-040-9
#5-8 ISBN - 978-1-59707-075-1
#9-12 ISBN - 978-1-59707-125-3
All: Full-color, $29.95

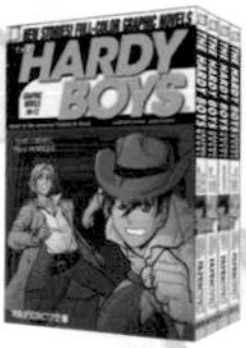
HARDY BOYS

CLASSICS Illustrated

Featuring Stories by the World's Greatest Authors

#1 "Great Expectations"
ISBN - 978-1-59707-097-3
#2 "The Invisible Man"
ISBN - 978-1-59707-106-2
#3 "Through the Looking-Glass"
ISBN - 978-1-59707-115-4
#4 "The Raven and Other Poems"
ISBN - 978-1-59707-140-6
NEW! #5 "Hamlet"
ISBN - 978-1-59707-149-9
All: 6 1/2 x 9, 56 pp., full-color, $9.95, hardcover

NEW!

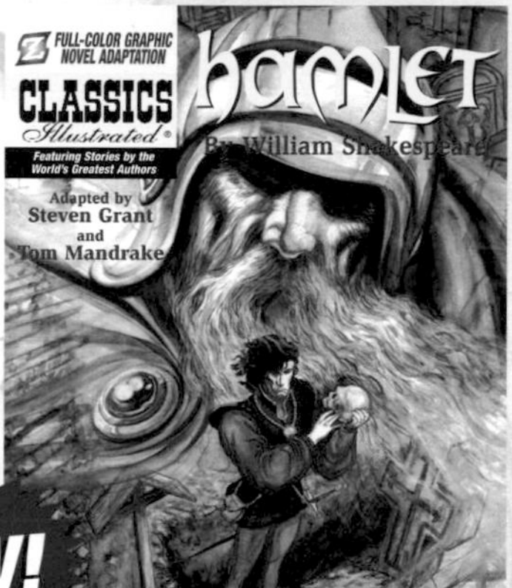
FULL-COLOR GRAPHIC NOVEL ADAPTATION
CLASSICS Illustrated
Featuring Stories by the World's Greatest Authors
Hamlet
By William Shakespeare
Adapted by
Steven Grant
and
Tom Mandrake
PAPERCUTZ

Please add $4.00 postage and handling. Add $1.00 for each additional item.
Make check payable to NBM publishing. Send To:
Papercutz, 40 Exchange Place, Suite 1308,
New York, New York 10005, 1-800-886-1223
www.papercutz.com

NANCY DREW girl detective
AND
THE HARDY BOYS
NOW READ THEIR ADVENTURES ON YOUR MOBILE PHONE!
ALSO AVAILABLE FOR iPHONE!
ON THE WEB:
WWW.GOCOMICS.COM/COMICBOOKS
ON YOUR MOBILE PHONE:
M.GOCOMICS.COM
gocomics™
PAPERCUTZ

WATCH OUT FOR PAPERCUTZ™

Welcome to the Backpages of NANCY DREW Graphic Novel #17 "City Under the Basement." I'm Jim Salicrup, Boy Editor (-in-Chief) of Papercutz, the publisher of all sorts of cool graphic novels. In these Backpages, we tell you all the exciting things going on at Papercutz, and there's so much to report, we better get right to it before we run out of room!

First, as you noticed, this volume of NANCY DREW is the second and concluding part of "The Secret Within." Back in NANCY DREW Graphic Novels #9 –11 we ran the three-part "The High Miles Mystery." What do you think about continued stories in the Papercutz NANCY DREW graphic novels? Love it? Hate it? Do you want each graphic novel to have one complete story? Do you want more continued stories? Or do you want a mix, like we're doing now? Please let us know!

Second, the best way to let us know what you think is to post a message on our blog at www.papercutz.com! Not only do NANCY DREW writers Stefan Petrucha and Sarah Kinney blog, we hope Sho Murase will be blogging there soon too!

Third, starting with #19 "Cliffhanger" our NANCY DREW Graphic Novels will have a bold, new look! Just as the Simon & Schuster ND novels have switched to a new logo, we'll be switching to the new bigger logo too! The covers may look different, but never fear -- the insides will still have the comics by Stefan Petrucha, Sarah Kinney, and Sho Murase that we all love so much!

Fourth, the April 3rd, 2009 issue of ENTERTAINMENT WEEKLY named Nancy Drew as one of their Top 20 Heroes! Nancy Drew came in at #17, beating out Batman, who had to settle for being #18! How cool is that? We already know how cool Nancy is -- it's nice to see EW recognize it too!

Fifth, we wanted to share some BIG NEWS with you! GERONIMO STILTON will be starring in an all-new series of big full-color graphic novels from Papercutz. The first two are coming your way in August – GERONIMO STILTON Graphic Novel #1 "The Discovery of America" and GERONIMO STILTON Graphic Novel #2 "The Secret of the Sphinx" – but we've got a special preview of GERONIMO STILTON Graphic Novel #1 "The Discovery of America" on the following pages!

Sixth, we also thought you'd might like a peek at TOTALLY SPIES! Graphic Novel #1 "The OP." If you haven't already picked up the four, fabulous full-color TOTALLY SPIES! Graphic Novels, they're all available right now at booksellers everywhere!

Finally, thanks for picking up this Papercutz graphic novel. We greatly appreciate your support. Talk to you on the Papercutz blog!

Thanks,

Jim

DON'T MISS GERONIMO STILTON GRAPHIC NOVEL #1 "THE DISCOVERY OF AMERICA" COMING IN AUGUST '09!

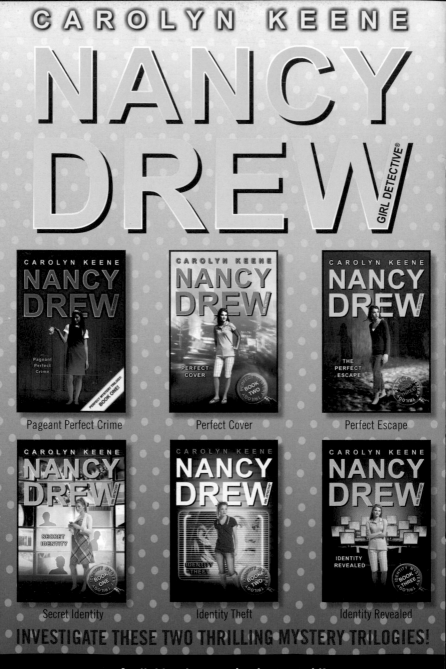

CAROLYN KEENE
NANCY DREW
GIRL DETECTIVE®

Pageant Perfect Crime

Perfect Cover

Perfect Escape

Secret Identity

Identity Theft

Identity Revealed

INVESTIGATE THESE TWO THRILLING MYSTERY TRILOGIES!

Uncover a Trail of Secrets and Sabotage in

NANCY DREW®
The White Wolf of Icicle Creek